The Rules

for

Hearts

BOOKS BY SARA RYAN

The Rules for Hearts

Me and Edith Head (with Steve Lieber)

Empress of the World

The Rules for Hearts

a family drama

Sara Ryan

VIKING

Author's note: Some places that I've written about in this book are real, though I've changed details and added elements to suit my story. But Forest House and all its inhabitants are fictional.

VIKING
Published by Penguin Group
Penguin Group (USA) Inc., 345 Hudson Street, New York, New York 10014, U.S.A.
Penguin Group (Canada), 90 Eglinton Avenue East, Suite 700, Toronto, Ontario, Canada M4P
2Y3 (a division of Pearson Penguin Canada Inc.)
Penguin Books Ltd, 80 Strand, London WC2R 0RL, England
Penguin Ireland, 25 St Stephen's Green, Dublin 2, Ireland
(a division of Penguin Books Ltd)
Penguin Group (Australia), 250 Camberwell Road, Camberwell, Victoria 3124, Australia (a
division of Pearson Australia Group Pty Ltd)
Penguin Books India Pvt Ltd, 11 Community Centre, Panchsheel Park,
New Delhi–110 017, India
Penguin Group (NZ), Cnr Airborne and Rosedale Roads, Albany, Auckland 1310, New Zealand
(a division of Pearson New Zealand Ltd)
Penguin Books (South Africa) (Pty) Ltd, 24 Sturdee Avenue, Rosebank, Johannesburg 2196,
South Africa

Penguin Books Ltd, Registered Offices: 80 Strand, London WC2R 0RL, England

First published in 2007 by Viking, a member of Penguin Group (USA) Inc.

1   3   5   7   9   10   8   6   4   2

Lyrics quoted on page 122 are from "Palmcorder Yajna" by the Mountain Goats, C & P Cadmean
Dawn [ASCAP], rights administered by Pacific Electric and used with permission of the artist.

LIBRARY OF CONGRESS CATALOGING-IN-PUBLICATION DATA IS AVAILABLE
ISBN: 978-0-670-05906-5

Printed in U.S.A.
Set in Goudy Old Style
Book design by Jim Hoover

for U. C., with love

CAST, IN ORDER OF APPEARANCE

BATTLE HALL DAVIES, *18-year-old high school graduate, accepted to Reed College*

NICHOLAS DAVIES, *22, Battle's older brother, a cab driver, resident of Forest House*

MERYL DAVENPORT, *22, swimming instructor, resident of Forest House*

AURORA KNEEDLER, *46, owner of Forest House and artistic director of Theater Borealis*

ROBERT CRACKNELL, *50, resident of Forest House, set designer and builder, Aurora's partner*

CHARLES FAHEY, *27, gardener, bike messenger, designer, resident of Forest House*

HENRY O'BRIAN, *55, donor to and actor in Theater Borealis*

DAMIAN J. WOLF, *28, actor in Theater Borealis*

ANNALISA TANNAHILL, *34, actor in Theater Borealis*

ELLERY TANNAHILL-LIPPMAN, *11, Annalisa's daughter, actor in Theater Borealis*

THE MINIONS, *assorted genders, ages, Robert's helpers in the Theater Borealis scene shop*

LUCKY, *3, a dog*

The Rules

for

Hearts

PROLOGUE

Church basement, Chapel Hill,
North Carolina, almost five years ago

IT'S BINGO NIGHT. My brother, Nick, and I are in the
youth room next to the social hall, playing hearts. We always
play hearts on bingo night.

Dad used to be an actor, so he never needs a microphone,
whether he's preaching or calling the numbers. We hear him
boom, "O-69!"

We crack up.

Nick is sixteen, I'm thirteen, and he's my favorite person.
He's smarter and funnier and more charming than anyone.
He teaches me card tricks and dirty jokes. He says that ev-
eryone except me is a hypocrite, especially Mom and Dad.
He knows the best music, the best places to go, and he hardly
ever complains about his tagalong little sister.

Three weeks later, on his seventeenth birthday, he runs
away.

ACT I

Are You Lost?

scene i

IT'S MY FOURTH time around this block. I'm idling—
again—in front of an old purple house, almost invisible behind a tall, ivy-covered fence.

A dark-haired girl opens the gate, walks up to my car, and
taps on my window.

"Are you lost?" she asks.

I roll down the window and hand the girl a piece of paper.

"I'm looking for this address."

"You've found it. You must be Nick's sister, right?"

I nod, pull over, and park. My hands are shaking. I have
pictured the end of this trip since I pulled out of Mom and
Dad's driveway six days ago, but the scenes in my head never
included anyone but me and my brother.

I rub my eyes, rake my hands through what there is of my hair, open the car door, and get out.

"I'm Meryl," the dark-haired girl says. She holds out her hand. "One of the housemates."

"Battle," I say.

Meryl's curly black hair is escaping from a low ponytail tied with a bright orange ribbon. Her white T-shirt is snug under her faded green overalls, and I can see the muscles in her shoulders. When I take her hand, I feel a jolt I haven't felt in more than a year.

Uh-oh. I didn't picture this scene, either.

"I'll help you unload," Meryl says.

"Thank you. Um, do you happen to know where my brother is?"

It feels funny to say "my brother." It's not a phrase I've had much occasion to use for a while.

"Nope, no idea. Let's get your stuff onto the porch."

"Thanks, but I need to make a quick call first."

I'm dizzy with fatigue, but Mom and Dad need to hear that I've arrived safely.

They know I'm moving into a house with some people for the summer before I start at Reed College. I showed them the ad on the Internet.

They don't know that one of the people is their son.

I dial, the phone rings, the machine picks up. "Hey,

I'm here, I'm fine, I'll talk to you soon." I hang up.

The air feels soft. The sky is gray, with a few thin clouds, and something about the quality of the light makes the green of leaves and grass seem brighter.

"Okay, I've done my duty. Let me open the trunk," I say.

Meryl and I each grab a box. Meryl reads, "'Paperbacks, white bookshelf.' God, color-coordinated labels? *Sure* you're related to Nick?"

I smile. "It's just easier. You know."

"No"—Meryl shakes her head—"*easy* is when you throw everything into the back of the truck, floor it, and get the hell out of Dodge."

"I wouldn't know about that," I say.

But Nick would.

Meryl and I walk back and forth from the car to the porch, piling up boxes. My eyes swim and my balance is a little off, but I don't say anything. It's not Meryl's fault that my brother can't be bothered to meet me, when it's been four and a half years since I've seen him and I've driven across the country to move in with him.

Then I pick up one of the few boxes I've labeled FRAGILE, get halfway up the walk, and trip.

The box flies out of my hands, hits the ground, and opens. Styrofoam packing peanuts spill out, along with what they're protecting: two puppets, a boy and a girl. Some of them broke the girl's fall. But the boy landed right on the concrete walk.

"Are you okay?" Meryl asks.

"Fine." I squat to pick up the peanuts before the breeze sends them all over the neighborhood.

Meryl kneels to investigate the boy.

The little gold crown he'd worn has split in half.

"Hmm, this is kind of broken," she says.

"I think I'll be able to fix it." I nestle the puppets back into the box, then pick up the halves of the boy's crown.

They look like a charm, but for what?

I put the crown halves into the pocket of my hoodie, then pick up another box.

Once we've gotten everything out of my car, Meryl says, "Take the stereo faceplate, too. Or at least put it in the glove compartment."

"Okay." This doesn't look like a bad neighborhood. What am I not seeing?

I shove the faceplate into the glove compartment, on top of the trip planner that's gotten me from Chapel Hill to Portland.

"Smoke break," Meryl says, digging into the pocket of her overalls and retrieving a pack and a lighter.

"Don't worry, nobody smokes in the house," she adds, grinning to reveal small, crooked, slightly yellow teeth.

While Meryl smokes, I take a closer look at the purple house I'm moving into. It's old—Victorian maybe?—and huge, with lots of windows that have that ripply-looking glass.

Nick didn't even tell me how many people live here, just that I'd like them.

Where is he?

"So how long did it take you to get here?" Meryl asks.

"About a week. It would've been faster, but I stayed in hotels for a couple of nights."

"Swank."

I shake my head. "More like antiswank. This one place had a patch of fluorescent orange mold growing on the carpet."

"Ew, and you *stayed* there? I'd have left."

A cab screeches to a stop in front of the house. My pulse thuds in my throat. Nick drives a cab now, he told me.

"That's probably him now," Meryl says.

But it's a woman who steps out. She's about my mom's age, and it looks like she spends a lot of time on her eyebrows. They're perfectly arched. Her black hair is growing out, though—I see about an inch of gray roots.

She stomps up the porch steps. "I need nicotine."

She takes two cigarettes from Meryl's pack, puts one in her mouth, cups the other in her palm like a tiny doll. "Flame," she demands. Meryl leans in with her lighter.

"Oh, God," the woman says. "This day. This goddamn *day*. What is all this?"

She waves at my stuff, then notices me.

"Oh! Excuse me, you must be—what did Nick tell me your name was?"

"Battle."

"Excellent. A fierce name. We need more of those. Battle, I'm Aurora—*not* a fierce name, alas."

"But you make up for it," Meryl says.

"*Thank* you. Anyway, Battle, I'm Aurora, and I own this place. Welcome to Forest House."

"Thanks."

"If I were a good person, I'd help you move everything up into your room, but frankly, after the day I've had, the very *idea* exhausts me, so my proposal is that we wait for your lovely brother to turn up and make him do it."

"Okay. Can you tell me where a restroom is?"

"Past the kitchen on the left."

As soon as I step inside, I see why Aurora calls it Forest House. There are more plants here than I've ever seen inside a building, in pots, in hanging baskets, in planters—from African violets like the ones Grandma always had to rubber trees with branches that graze the ceiling. Jungle House would be more accurate.

Though a jungle wouldn't have so many books. Some are stacked on brick-and-board shelves, some are in teetery piles on the floor. It looks and smells like a greenhouse crossed with a used bookstore.

There are even plants growing inside the dirt-filled claw-foot tub. God, I hope there's another bathroom upstairs, and it's not that everyone in the house is opposed to bathing.

When I get back out to the porch, Aurora's in the middle of a sentence:

"—all over the damned play! Lovers and madmen. Love in idleness. The course of true love. Love love love love love. Blah blah blah, et cetera, et cetera."

Aurora looks up. "Battle! *You'll* bring a fresh perspective! Tell me: should I get married?"

"Um . . . to whom?"

"Mister Robert Cracknell. You'll meet him soon; he lives here, too. I hope that doesn't shock you."

"It doesn't." If anything, I'm shocked that she's asking my opinion after having known me for less than fifteen minutes.

"Good, because if it did, I'm sure you'd be far *more* shocked by . . . hmmm . . . well, never mind, you'll meet everyone soon enough. *Anyway*, Robert has asked me to marry him. I can't imagine how he could have even *thought* of asking me when he *knows* we're about to start *Midsummer*!"

"Hey, the show's all about the weddings," Meryl says.

Aurora sighs. "It is, and it isn't. It's really a lot about hierarchies, and overturning them—and how you don't come out of the forest unchanged—but it *is* about love and marriage, too, certainly. So I think it was very manipulative of him to make this . . . *proposition* just now. Don't you think so, Battle?"

"I couldn't say."

Where the hell is Nick?

"It's really the *idea* of marriage, how it shuts off all kinds of options, the idea of giving up forever those very first moments you have with someone new, before you've even kissed, when you just get that *connection*—"

Meryl grabs my hands and stares dreamily into my eyes. Aurora laughs and says, "Yes, exactly! When you're oblivious to the world, just absorbed in each other."

The way Meryl's hands feel almost takes my mind off my brother. I can't meet her eyes.

Meryl doesn't let go, and Aurora goes on, in an even softer, sweeter voice, "But you're not sure yet, you can't take anything for granted, I mean, what if you've misinterpreted all those signs you thought you saw? You can't know, until somebody makes that first move. . . ."

I feel hypnotized. I lean closer. Meryl leans toward me, too.

My brain isn't working. It's not telling me that it's crazy to be millimeters away from kissing a strange girl because an even stranger woman says she misses what it feels like to have a crush.

"Well, no introductions necessary, I see," my brother says.

The spell is broken. Meryl and I move away from each other, and I look up.

"Your hair's longer than mine," I say stupidly. "And you have earrings."

He's smiling. His face is thinner. He's got what looks like a three-day growth of beard, and there's something different about his eyes; they seem—what? Not tired. Not bloodshot.

Older?

"I can't believe you're really here!" he says. "God, when'd you get so tall?"

I haven't stopped being angry. "Sometime in the past four and a half years."

He crushes me into a hug, and after a frozen second, I put my arms around him and hug him back.

"Are you guys twins?" Meryl asks. "You look alike."

A strangled sound, not quite a laugh, not quite a cough, comes out of my throat.

Nick says, "Sure."

"No, we're not." I step out of the hug. "Nick, I have a present for you."

The last few weeks before I left, I went all over Chapel Hill taking pictures of everywhere we used to go together. Some things had changed, of course, but I figured he'd want to know that, too.

I find the box labeled MEMENTOS, ETC., open it, and take out the album. I used archival paper and acid-free photo corners. The cover is dark forest green, his favorite color. Or at least it used to be.

"Here," I say.

Nick opens it, flips quickly from page to page, a slight, vague smile on his face.

It's only then that it occurs to me that making a scrapbook of the place my brother ran away from was not, perhaps, my most brilliant idea ever.

"You spent a lot of time on that," he says. "I can tell."

Then he sets the album down and reaches into a paper bag.

"Got a present for you, too."

He hands me a six-pack of Pabst, smiling the way he always used to when he'd give me a Coke that he'd shaken up.

I pull out a can, pop the top. The beer geysers up out of the can, spilling over my hands and arms. Nick laughs and applauds.

"He's always doing that. I thought you'd have known," Meryl says.

"Oh, *thanks*!" I say. I grab for Nick and make sure to wet his jacket and T-shirt while I hug him again, inhaling the malty scent of beer.

"You're welcome," he says. Getting dampened with beer doesn't appear to bother him.

I raise my can to him and take a sip.

"Y'all should have some, too," I say. "Though you might want to let it sit a minute."

Aurora, Meryl, and Nick all take cans.

A stocky, bearded man pushes open the gate, walks up the steps, and glares at us. He looks at Aurora. "Enjoying yourself?"

"Robert, this is our new housemate, Nick's sister. Her name is Battle."

The man shifts his glare to me. "Hello, Battle. If I were you, I'd get my crap off the porch before I started partying. But"—he sniffs the air, wrinkles his nose—"I guess it's a little late for that. If you'll excuse me."

He goes past us into the house.

What a great first impression. Thanks, Nick.

Meryl whistles. "Stay out of *his* way. Go be nice to him, Aurora."

Aurora says, "I most certainly will *not*. He was extremely rude. Battle, I must apologize on his behalf."

I set down the beer. "Will someone show me where my room is?"

"Absolutely," says my brother. "And we'll all help carry up the boxes, right?" He smiles at Aurora and Meryl.

"You don't have to," I say. "I can do it."

"No worries," says Meryl. "You don't have that much stuff. We can bucket-brigade it."

And that's what we do—each box goes from Aurora on the porch, to Meryl in the middle of the living room, to me at the foot of the stairs, to Nick at the doorway of my new room. Despite the supposed efficiency, I'm the only one running up and down the stairs, but I don't mind. I've been on the road for days, and my legs welcome the work.

Once Meryl has passed the last box (HARDBACKS) to me, she and Aurora disappear, and I carry it up the stairs to the door where Nick's waiting. I'm sweating a little and breathing fast.

"Behold!" Nick says, pushing the door open with one foot. My new room is small, with freshly painted white walls, a scuffed, scratched dark wood floor, and a tiny closet with nothing in it but three empty hangers and a blue baseball cap hanging from a nail. The room has one big open window that looks out onto the back garden. I set down the last box. My arms feel a little rubbery, in that way that happens when you're suddenly no longer carrying something heavy.

I sit on the windowsill and, holding on with one hand, lean backward out of the window, feeling the slight breeze move through my hair.

"Nice view, huh?" Nick says.

"Yeah," I say, halfway upside down. I see that Meryl and Aurora are in the backyard, talking and gesturing with their cigarettes, too far away for me to hear.

"Glad you're here," Nick says. "I wasn't sure you were going to make it."

"Why not?"

"Parental controls."

I laugh. I had to learn how to disable those back when I started IMing, and somewhere along the line, I'd turned the phrase into shorthand for every form of discipline Mom and Dad imposed.

I pull myself upright. "It wasn't a big deal," I lie. "I said I wanted to get to know the area before school started, the end. It's not like I said, 'Oh, by the way, last year Nick tracked me down on the Internet and told me I should go to Reed, and that's why I chose that school, and now I'm moving in with him for the summer.' As far as they know, you're still in New York working on that show or whatever you said on the postcard. That was what, nine or ten months ago? I told you how Mom cried when it came. You should call them. It would make them really happy."

"Don't be too sure about that. Hey, we left the beer on the porch. I don't know about you, but I could sure use another one."

I'd rather start to unpack, but I follow my brother back down to the porch. Red and yellow petals are falling from the sky.

I look up. There's a guy on the second-story balcony dead-heading rosebushes. He's slight, with spiky blue hair.

"Were you sleeping up there again, you slacker?" Nick calls up to him.

The guy grins, pinches off some more dead blooms, and aims them at Nick's head.

"C'mon down! You need to meet my sister!"

The guy climbs up onto the porch railing, grabs a thick nearby branch, and swings out into the tree. He's barefoot. It doesn't take him long to get to the ground. He looks like some new blue-crested species of monkey.

"Hi! I'm Charles."

"I'm Battle. That was impressive."

"Just faster than going through the house. Nice to meet you!"

"Charles is a man of many talents," Nick says, smiling. "Cooking's another. Speaking of which, you should get going on dinner, dude—Battle's been on the road all day."

"If you help, it'll be ready that much sooner."

Nick shakes his head. "No, we're exhausted. We're going to take a moment for a beverage. But we'll so appreciate dinner when it's ready," he says, sounding like he means it. He flashes Charles a smile, and Charles shakes his head, but then goes into the house.

Drinking more will confirm Robert's rapidly formed opinion of me, but I'm hot and tired and thirsty, and the beer's still cold.

Nick and I sit next to each other on the porch swing. Nearby there's a coffee can full of cigarette butts and sand. I wonder how often someone kicks it over.

Then I really look at Nick, trying to see how he's changed.

He won't talk to Mom and Dad; he's been clear on that since he first found me online. It was only after I harassed him for weeks that he finally sent them that one postcard from New York, right before he moved to Portland. Dad almost ripped it up, but Mom stopped him. I think it's still on the refrigerator.

When Nick and I IM, mostly he tells me funny stories about the people who ride in his cab. He's never said why he ran away, what happened between the time he left North Carolina and when he got to New York, how (and why) he went from New York to Portland, how he acquired a cab driver's license.

But then, I haven't asked.

Charles sticks his blue head out the front door. "Dinner in about five, you two."

"You are the true and living God," Nick says, and we follow Charles into the kitchen.

Robert and Aurora are at opposite ends of the long rectangular wooden table. It has benches on either side, instead of chairs, and looks like it was maybe designed as outdoor furniture. Nick sits across from Meryl. Charles fills a bowl for me, and I sit between Meryl and Aurora.

"So, what brings you to Portland?" Robert asks, looking at my beer, not me. He sounds like he wants to ask, "What would it take to make you leave?"

"I'll be starting at Reed this fall," I say.

"Figures," Robert says.

"Fuckin' Reedies," Charles says, but he's smiling, and I choose to interpret the comment as friendly.

Charles's dinner is fantastic: stir-fried spicy tofu, broccoli lightly steamed with a little garlic and lemon, served over the best brown rice I've ever had. It's like an antidote to the beer, and I feel more human, less like I'm going to collapse.

"Reed is an *excellent* school," Aurora says, glaring at Robert.

"She's a supergenius," Nick says. "She's gonna save all the little baby animals."

I used to think I wanted to be a vet. Then one of my dogs got hurt. I asked if I could watch the vet while he worked. He said yes.

I threw up.

"Shut up." I reach across the table to punch Nick on the arm.

Meryl says, "Now, kids, play nice."

Nick says, "No way. We've got a lot of sibling rivalry to catch up on." He grins at me.

Is that why I'm here?

When everyone's finished eating, I offer to do the dishes because it seems like the right thing to do. Aurora and Robert argue their way upstairs, and Meryl just leaves the house, without telling anyone where she's going.

Nick and Charles stay in the kitchen while I work. After a few minutes, Charles gets up from the table and starts drying.

"Hey, you shouldn't be doing that," Nick says to Charles. "You cooked!"

"Well, I didn't see you about to pick up the dishrag—be my guest," Charles says, tossing the wet rag at my brother. Nick tosses it back.

"No, no, you two have a good rhythm going. It's a pleasure to watch you work."

Nick stretches out on one of the benches and smiles. He's not that tall, and he's certainly not fat, but somehow, he still takes up a lot of space in the room.

Charles and I finish the dishes.

"So, I've got to work, but I can drop you guys off at the grocery first," Nick says.

I'd rather get back up to my room, unpack a little, and crash. But the way Nick says it makes me think that buying groceries is something that's required of me as a new member of the household, so I don't protest.

Charles and I climb into Nick's cab, and I have to plug my nose. "God, Nick," I say, "it smells like something died back here—what the hell?"

"You don't want to know. Just roll down the windows; it won't be much longer."

"Ask him about his worst fare," Charles says.

"What, you mean *you?*" Nick asks.

I already know the story of his worst fare—some guy who drunkenly expounded about his political philosophy for forty-five minutes while Nick drove him into the hinterlands. Then he relieved himself on the seat, and proved not to have a wallet. That was one of the first stories Nick told me when he tracked me down—after he'd verified his identity by telling me my middle name (Hall—after the building where our parents met), the color of the carpet in our living room (a trick question: a Persian rug), and Dad's favorite part of the Bible (the Song of Songs, always embarrassing).

It disturbed me how quickly I got used to being in touch again, and how much I'd worry when days would go by and I didn't hear from him.

I squint at Nick's cab-driver ID. His hair's shorter, his earrings aren't in, and he's wearing a button-down. "You look old in that picture."

"That's 'cause I *am* old."

"How late are you working tonight?" Charles asks.

"As long as they need me."

"Mister Overtime over here."

"Hey, once the show starts, I won't be able to take many shifts. I need to get in a lot of hours before then."

"The show Aurora and Meryl were talking about before?" I ask.

"You didn't tell her?" Charles asks.

Nick stops in front of a Safeway. "Here you go. See y'all later. Battle, don't believe a word he says."

I watch my brother pull back out into traffic.

"So, what should I not believe you about?"

Charles puts an arm around me and smiles. "Never mind. Let's buy groceries. You push the cart and I'll fill it."

"Okay."

"We used to rotate the grocery shopping, but after a few too many nights of ramen, box mac and cheese, and frozen pizza, I took it upon myself."

Charles removes a peach from the sweet-smelling pyramid near the front of the store and squeezes it gently, then nods and puts it into the cart.

"So, how does that work?" I ask. "You don't just pay for all the food?"

"Oh, God, no. Everyone chips in. Well, that's the theory, anyway."

I take out my wallet. "How much do you need for today?"

"Twenty?"

"Okay. What else am I responsible for?"

Charles scoops baby spinach into a plastic bag. "I take it you haven't gotten the rundown about how Forest House operates?"

Nick said it was kind of like a co-op, so I looked up co-ops online, but I kept finding contradictory information, and I lost four hours reading a year's worth of house meeting minutes from someplace in the Midwest. They wanted to kick this one guy out for never doing chores or showing up to meetings. But since he never showed up to meetings, it took them most of the year.

"I know how much rent is, but I don't know, like, who I pay or anything."

Charles twirls the bag of spinach and then ties a knot at the top.

"You are extremely lucky," he says. "You pay Aurora instead of an evil property-management company. And you didn't hear it from me, but she's been known to forget about charging. She owns Forest House outright, so the rent is gravy. Your brother collects for utilities. Oh, and breakfast and lunch are usually individual, but we all switch off cooking dinner."

"What do Robert and Meryl do?"

"In the house, or to pay the rent?"

"Both, I guess."

"Meryl teaches swimming at a community center. She cleans the bathrooms. Robert's a system administrator. He sweeps and mops. And you, by the way, will be dealing with recycling."

"Okay. Um, what about you?"

"Well, let's see. To pay the bills, I'm the world's oldest bike messenger, as long as my knees hold out. In the house, it's grocery shopping and gardening."

World's oldest? He's not old.

"For the house . . . are there, like, meetings?"

Charles laughs. "Not really, no. Between Forest House and the theater, we all spend more than enough time together."

"Is that how you all met?"

"Yep."

I'm trying not to be upset that Charles is the one to share all this useful information with me, and that Nick didn't bother to get time off for my first day in town, but I tell myself that it's good that he has a job. I can just hear Dad making some snide comment about how it's about time Nick developed a work ethic.

Meanwhile we've been making our way around the Safeway, accumulating an assortment of healthier food than I would have thought a group of people my age would voluntarily purchase. Then again, I guess none of them *are* my age.

"How old are you?" I ask Charles.

"Don't worry, I've got ID," he assures me. Among the healthy food items are a few bottles of cheap red wine.

"That's not why, I just wanted to know."

"How old do you think I am?" he asks.

The blue hair and the lip ring make it harder to tell.

"Twenty?"

"Twenty-seven."

Nine years older than me. Six years older than Nick.

How old is Meryl?

I try not to look nervous when the cashier rings up the wine. Charles gets carded, but she doesn't ask me to show mine. Maybe the bags under my eyes help.

"How do we get this back to the house?"

"We'll take the bus—it gets us within a few blocks."

Why didn't I just drive?

Oh, right. I wanted to see my brother.

The bus smells better than Nick's cab. Charles and I and our groceries sit near the back. It's not very crowded. I see five people reading. They all have chunky, black-framed glasses. Everyone on the bus looks a little dishevelled, like they all woke up late after sleeping in their clothes and had to leave the house without showering. On several people, this is a surprisingly good look.

"So, did you grow up in Portland?" I ask Charles.

He shakes his head. "I've lived a lot of places," he says vaguely.

I nod. I can't think of anything to say after that, and it seems like he can't, either, or maybe he just doesn't want to talk. Which is fine—I don't always want to talk, either. But a few times, I catch him looking hard at me. It's not like he's checking me out, more like he's trying to *figure* me out. Each time I see him doing it, he looks away.

I'm crashing. I've just closed my eyes when Charles says, "This is our stop." I make myself get up, sleepwalk the four blocks back to Forest House, and help him put the groceries away. Then I stagger up the stairs to my new room.

But before I can go to sleep, I have to inflate my air mattress and find the box with sheets and pillowcases in it. I bought the air mattress because I knew I was only going to be here for a couple of months before orientation, and there'll be a bed in my dorm room. Besides the air mattress, my "furniture" is two folding bookcases, two cardboard dressers, and a folding laundry hamper. Not classy, but it all fit in my car. And I kind of love how temporary it is.

I miss my dogs, Dante and Beatrice. But I always miss them in the summers.

I've spent the past three summers away from my dogs—and Mom and Dad. On the surface, that seems like the opposite of what would happen. One of your children runs away, so you send the other one to camp for three months?

I don't know. Maybe they thought I should expand my horizons. The first year it was a ballet camp, which I loathed, and then the next two years, it was the Siegel Summer Institute for Gifted and Talented Youth.

Which expanded my horizons a lot more than Mom and Dad had bargained for.

scene ii

THERE'S A GREEN *blur all around me, and I'm trying to get out, but leaves keep curling around my arms and legs, and then a tendril works its way up my nose, cutting off my breathing—*

My eyes open. Then Nick takes his fingers out of my nose and wipes them off on his pants, giggling.

"God!" I say, rubbing my nose with the back of my hand. "I can't believe you still *do* that!"

"Figured it'd still be the fastest way to wake you up, and I was right, wasn't I? Listen, I need you to help me with something."

I blink and squint at the clock. It's not even six yet. "Does it involve my coming into contact with anyone else's snot, or vice versa?"

"Possibly. C'mon, we've gotta be done before my next shift starts."

"I need a shower."

"No, you don't," Nick says, bouncing up and down on the edge of my bed. "You'll want one afterward, though."

"What are we doing?"

"Picking up some stuff."

"Why will I need a shower?"

"'Cause girls are funny that way."

I glare at him. "Right. Get out, I'm going to get dressed."

When I get downstairs, four and a half minutes later, Nick holds a glass out to me. "I don't know if you still like it."

I take a sip and smile.

"Man, I haven't tasted this in years."

It's chocolate milk with a splash of coffee, poured over ice, with cinnamon dusted on top. I smile again and drink more, happy to be standing in a sunny, plant-filled kitchen with my brother, who remembers my favorite drink from before I learned to take my coffee black.

Nick punches me lightly on the arm. "Okay, let's hit it. You can take that with you."

Today, we take my car.

"Have you got bungee cords?" Nick asks.

"Um, I just moved across the country, in case you forgot. I doubt there's a bungee cord left in Chapel Hill—they're all here in my car."

"Good."

Nick directs me to make a seemingly arbitrary series of right and left turns on tree-lined streets, until we get to a corner where there's a little beige house with an American flag in the window and a sign saying NO JUSTICE, NO PEACE.

"Excellent!" Nick says. "I was afraid someone else would've snagged them by now."

On the curb next to the little beige house are a dirty gray velour couch, listing to one side because one of its legs has broken off, and a blue plaid armchair that looks only a little less the worse for wear than the couch. Nick sprints out of the car and sprawls into the chair, putting his feet up on the couch.

"Don't tell me you're still into Dumpster décor," I say. I can't count the number of times Mom yelled at him for bringing something home from someone's trash. She wasn't crazy about it when he picked up clothes at the church rummage sale, either, but that was harder for her to complain about.

"Okay, I won't tell you," Nick says, smiling.

I cross my arms over my chest. "Bugs! Millions and millions of bugs!"

Nick scratches himself furiously, then settles further into the chair, putting his hands behind his head and grinning.

"Gross," I say.

"Free," he says.

"Where're you going to *put* them?"

"Couch in the living room. Chair in my room. I've been needing one."

"You think Aurora's going to want that couch in her house?"

Nick laughs. "You don't know her very well yet."

"It's broken, didn't you notice?" I point at the corner of the couch with the missing leg.

"That's *so* easy to fix. You just need a piece of wood that's the same height."

"I wish I had gloves."

"Told you you'd want to shower afterward," Nick says, shifting to drape himself sideways across the chair.

"Okay. So how do you want to do this?" I demand.

"Easy. Bungee-cord the couch up there"—Nick points at my car's roof, like he's directing—"and the chair will fit in the trunk."

"That would more or less require you to get *out* of it," I say.

Nick springs up. "You're so right. Okay, open the trunk and then grab the other end. We're going to have to flip it—see, it's only gonna fit if we shove it in going the other way. . . ."

"Right."

Nick pushes. The chair leg collides with the trunk lid, making a horrible screech, scratching the paint. I pull it away, and that snags the chair's upholstery. Nick shoves again and manages to wedge it in.

"Ha!" he says. "Okay, that was the easy part."

He points to the couch.

I wince.

"Come on. Reduce, reuse, recycle."

"We'll never get it onto the roof."

"Take the cushions off, that'll help."

"Right, because cushions are so heavy."

Nick puts the cushions in the backseat, then reaches into the crevice of the couch and smiles.

"See, we're making money!" He holds up a quarter. "Who knows what else could be buried in here?"

"Exactly my point. Let's just take the chair, okay?"

"Cushions are already in the car."

"Fine, we can take the cushions. But there's no way that's making it onto the roof. Not to mention that it's *broken*!"

"Oh, and we *couldn't* have anything less than pristine in our perfect home, now could we?"

"It's broken, it's probably infested, it's disgusting. I don't know why you want it."

"Would you get the fuck over yourself, princess? *You* might still be used to it, but I don't get to just ask Mommy and Daddy to *buy* me everything I want. So don't you fucking judge me." Nick shoves the quarter into his pocket.

I feel like a fly who's just been swatted with a Buick.

"I was judging the damn *couch*. But go ahead, take it. You can get my car detailed after the rest of the paint comes off."

"Unscrew the legs and put them in the backseat. Nothing else on there will mess up your precious, precious paint job."

The couch slides up as smoothly as a sled.

"See?" Nick smiles, and it's as though he was never angry. "You just need to trust me."

He tosses a bungee cord across the roof, but it comes too fast for me to catch it, and it bounces off my cheek and hits the side of the car. I bend over and clutch my cheek. It stings like crazy.

"Ow! God! You could've put my eye out!"

"Are you okay? God, I really nailed you there, didn't I?"

He comes over to me, takes my face in his hands. "Let me see . . . it's a little red, but I think you'll be all right. Want to sit down a minute?"

"No. But I want you to drive." I hand him the keys.

Nick moves the seat back, even though we're pretty close to the same height. The first time he stops for a stop sign, he says, "Your brakes are squishy. You should get those looked at."

"I have to get a job first." I rub my cheek. "How old d'you have to be to drive a cab?"

"Older than you."

We ride in silence for a while. I close my eyes.

"Charles said everyone in the house does theater."

"Yup. Theater Borealis. Aurora's in charge. As you might guess from the name."

"Cute. You've been in a lot of shows?"

He never messaged me about acting.

Nick nods. "I'm indispensable."

"Really."

"Yeah. Once we're in rehearsal, you won't be seeing me much."

"Oh, good," I say. "Because God knows I'm already sick of you."

Right then, I decide to audition.

scene iii

THE NEIGHBORHOOD CLOSEST to the theater is jammed with expensive stores. I walk through it, an hour or so before auditions are scheduled to begin, in a sort of trance. I took the bus, because Charles told me it was impossible to find parking in this part of town. And I'm by myself, because I didn't want to have to talk to anyone.

The people walking around here look polished and sleek. They have glossier hair and newer-looking shoes than the people on the bus. Lots of them are talking on tiny, shiny cell phones. Some of them look like they're in a huge rush, and others like they have all the time and money in the world.

I register isolated objects from the window displays:

A pair of pointy, cream-colored stilettos with brown top-stitching.

Black chunky glasses frames, like the ones the people on

the bus were wearing, next to an antique Underwood type-writer.

An orange polyester A-line dress from the seventies that's so ugly I can't stop looking at it.

I try going over my audition speech in my head, but I can't focus.

Why am I doing this? Shouldn't I be looking for a *job*?

That was part of my agreement with Mom and Dad. If I was going to be permitted to move out of their house and across the country three months early, I needed to be doing something productive. Ideally, they'd have liked me to get an internship, but it's a bit difficult when you have very little idea what you might want to intern *as*.

So, I need a job. Some kind of a job.

But right now, I'm going to walk into the theater and wait for my turn to audition.

It's an old building. The carpet is worn and stained in places; the ornamental molded plaster ceiling is pockmarked with water damage. It looks like it used to be a church, since the seats are pews. Which, of course, makes me think of Dad.

There's a lot we disagree about—Nick, for one thing—but I do have to give Dad a little credit. When he decided to become a minister, he didn't decide that all theater, everywhere, was corrupt and evil. He just decided that for him, "the pulpit was the best stage."

The pews—seats—here are about half full. Some people are muttering to themselves, others are chatting, others are stretching like athletes before a race, still others are looking at the ceiling or the floor. A few are wearing headphones. There's a little boy who can't be more than six or seven doing cartwheels down the central aisle, giggling all the way. A big white-bearded man in a seersucker suit, who looks like a fashion-conscious ogre, scoops him up, hoists him onto his shoulders, and takes him for a stroll. The boy shrieks with delight.

"Hey, housemate," Meryl says, sitting down next to me. "What are you doing here?"

Couldn't she have guessed? "Auditioning. You?"

"Oh, yeah. It's my favorite Shakespeare. I can't wait to see what Aurora's going to do with it."

"You want to do this for real?" I ask. "For a living?"

Meryl shrugs. "Dunno. If I was really serious about theater, I wouldn't be in Portland, I'd be in New York or Chicago, or *maybe* San Francisco—I hear there's some good stuff going on there. But I like Aurora, and I like living here, so . . . Do you want to be an actress?"

"I don't know, either."

I have no idea what I want to be. All I know is that at the end of the summer, I'm going to start college, and then, sometime in the next four years, figure out what comes next.

Just then Aurora sweeps in, beatnik-medieval in a bright blue silk head scarf, a long black dress, and high-heeled blue boots. She climbs the stairs to the stage and stands there for a minute, smiling. Then it's quiet.

"Thank you all for coming to the auditions for the Theater Borealis production of *A Midsummer Night's Dream*. I'm delighted to see so many people here to audition tonight, and I just want to ask all of you right now to please be patient, everyone will get a chance, but we'll certainly be here for a while."

I hear someone close by mutter, "Yeah, we'll be here for a while before she casts the exact same people as always."

"Shh," whispers the person next to the mutterer. "No negative thoughts!"

"Not negative, just accurate."

The only good part of last year was when I played Rosalind in our school's production of *As You Like It*. Unlike my ballet teacher, the director was delighted with my hair. I shaved my head last summer—the summer when so much else happened—and it'd only grown out a couple of inches when I auditioned, a week after I quit ballet. Gilbert, my director, said, "Your look is completely in sync with my vision!"

His Vision (although he used longer words to explain it): Rosalind was kind of odd.

My hair's still short, though according to my friend

Katrina, the style has shifted from "probably military" to "post-punk soft butch."

Three women in a row do the same monologue. I don't recognize it. But by the time the fourth fumbles it midway through, I'm drumming my fingers on my knees, mouthing the next line to prompt her.

Meryl grabs my hand. "Stop it, that's distracting." She squeezes my hand roughly, then lets it go.

Now it's Nick's turn. I hadn't spotted him in the audience; he must have come in without my noticing. He sits on the edge of the stage and says, without taking a pose or clearing his throat, "Be absolute for death; either death or life shall thereby be the sweeter. Reason thus with life; If I do lose thee, I do lose a thing that none but fools would keep. . . ."

He calls the audience death's fool, accuses us of fearing a poor worm, explains matter-of-factly that we aren't happy because we want what we don't have and forget what we have, and that even if we're rich, we're poor, because we'll only have our wealth for a short time before we die. It's a grim speech, but Nick seems to find it funny, and he makes everyone else think so, too.

Then he reads from *Midsummer*—Puck's speech that starts "Thou speak'st aright—I am that merry wanderer of the night"—and it doesn't sound like reading, it just sounds like he's telling everyone who he is. When he's done, I want to applaud.

"Thank you," says Aurora, sounding the same as she has when she's thanked everyone else who's auditioned so far. Nick leaps off the stage, and I think he's going to hurt himself, but he lands like a gymnast.

Meryl's next, and she—or rather, the person whose lines she's saying—is irritated with Claudio. He used to be plainspoken and warlike, but now he's interested in dancing and will lie awake for ten nights thinking about how to design some new fashionable piece of clothing, all because he's fallen in love. She paces, she imitates Claudio's ridiculous new airs. Then, suddenly, she stops, looks straight out into the audience, and asks, "May I be so converted and see with these eyes?"

She pauses, for a long time. Does she expect someone to answer? Then she goes on, concluding that love might turn her to an oyster, but that until all graces are united in one woman, she'll be safe from love. She enumerates the graces: wealth, wisdom, virtue, beauty, mildness, nobility, wit, and musicianship. The only thing that doesn't concern her is the color of the woman's hair.

She says the last line looking right at me.

Meryl's performance delights the ogre in seersucker. He has a loud, carrying laugh that almost drowns out Aurora's "Thank you."

I decide to step outside so I can concentrate. Meryl follows me.

"Did I put you to sleep?"

"Oh, no, not at all. But right now I just need a minute, okay?"

"Sure." Meryl walks a few feet away and lights a cigarette.

As soon as I'm by myself, I'm thinking about a girl. She was shocked when she heard I was going to play Rosalind—"I thought you only liked being onstage when you didn't have to talk. Dancing, I mean."

Nicola Lancaster. Nic. We met last summer at the Siegel Institute for Gifted and Talented Youth.

Though the word *met* doesn't come close to covering it.

She's sort of why I shaved my head, and sort of why my senior year, except for the play, was ass.

She turned me into an oyster.

I shut my eyes again.

WHEN I WALK back into the theater, it's almost empty. Meryl sits cross-legged on the floor. Nick's in the center aisle near the front of the theater, yawning and stretching. Aurora's scribbling in a notebook.

"We were about to send out a search party," Nick says.

"Can I—" I start, then stop.

Aurora glances up from her notes.

"Is it too late to audition?"

She looks hard at me.

"I called your name already."

Nick says, "Ah, come on. Cut her some slack—she's new."

Aurora scowls, but finally nods. "All right. Let's see if it runs in the family."

I wonder if Nick's told her about our dad, the actor turned preacher. I doubt it.

The stage seems much farther away than it did a minute ago. I think of sitting on the edge, but then I'd just be copying Nick, and if I stride around, I'll be copying Meryl.

I take a deep breath.

The speech I picked, which is probably too short, is from Act III. Rosalind is disguised as the youth Ganymede, telling Orlando—the man who loves her, Rosalind, not R-as-G—that he, Ganymede, can cure love. He'll do this by pretending to be the woman Orlando is in love with—who, of course, she really is—and being "changeable, longing and liking, proud, fantastical, apish, shallow, inconstant, full of tears, full of smiles."

In short, by driving him crazy.

"And this way will I take upon me," I say, fixing my eyes on an empty pew, "to wash your liver as clean as a sound sheep's heart, that there shall not be one spot of love in't."

That was way too fast. Gilbert always said to slow it down, let the audience appreciate the language.

And I didn't move enough.

Nick applauds. "Hey, when'd you learn that speech?"

"I told you. Last year."

Meryl says, "Shakespeare can be so gross. Sheep's hearts and livers, yeesh."

"Thank you," says Aurora. "I'll want to hear you read from the show, too, of course, but let's do that another time." She smiles. "I know where you live."

AFTER WE GET back from the theater, Aurora retreats to the attic. I go into the kitchen to get some water, and through the window over the sink, I can see Charles doing something in the back garden. Nick and Meryl join Robert to watch some cop show in the living room, but I'm not in the mood for TV, so I head upstairs. I get online, but no one's on that I want to talk to.

So I get in bed and lie there for a while listening to music, but I can't sleep. I start hearing irregular thumping and gasping sounds from somewhere in the house—it could be fighting, it could be sex. Either way, I'd rather not know.

Sometime after two, I give up, get dressed, and make my way downstairs, wincing at the loud creak of a step, flinching as a frond grazes my cheek. Tiptoe through the living room, slip out the front door. Then I get in the car, turn on the dome light, get out my Thomas Guide—this giant book that's a map of the whole city—and figure out how to get to the place where I'll be spending the next four years.

The streets are quiet—an occasional truck, a few bicyclists. I stop for a red light and see a couple arguing on a corner.

I park at the entrance. Am I trespassing, since I'm not a student yet? I don't care. I get out of the car and start walking. The sky is a purply blue. There are lots of big trees. Campus buildings loom, not ominous, but imposing in the dark.

And suddenly in my head, it's last summer.

I'm convinced that any second, I'll hear Katrina yelling about something we have to do *right* fucking *now*, or see Kevin looking all goofy with his Hacky Sack.

Or Nic.

With that little smile she'd always get when she saw me.

Then I'm replaying the night she and I spent in the woods, figuring out how to fit ourselves together.

I force myself back to the present, keep walking. Hear music, or something like it, and then see someone sitting under a tree with a banjo. After a minute, I recognize the song: it's the Misfits, "All Hell Breaks Loose." Isaac put it on a mix he sent me a while back. I'm glad this is the kind of place where people play old punk songs on banjos in the middle of the night.

In the distance, I see two lines of blue lights. As I get closer I see that they're illuminating a bridge, and it's not two lines of lights after all, but one. The second line is the lights' reflection in the water below.

I stand on the bridge, watching the way the water makes the lights seem to move. How many more times will I stand here? Who'll be with me?

The blue lights swim in front of my eyes.

ACT II

Some Very Interesting Choices

scene i

TWO DAYS LATER, at breakfast, Aurora says, "Usually, I'd be more formal about this and call you, but since you all live here—and you all *are* here, which is more surprising—I would like to offer you the part of Helena, you the part of Hermia, and you the part of Puck."

She points first at me, then Meryl, then Nick.

"Really? Awesome! It's not just 'cause I'm short, is it?" Meryl asks.

Aurora shakes her head, smiling.

Nick says, "Let me think about it. I've got a lot going on."

"Then why did you audition?" Meryl asks.

At the same time, Aurora says, "Think fast. You know that the first rehearsal's tomorrow night."

In the silence that follows, I say, "Thanks. I hope I'll do okay."

"I'm looking forward to it," Aurora says. "But I must say, this is a record—it's the most cast members in Forest House that we've ever had. I'm sure you'll all be horribly sick of each other by the first performance. Avoiding each other on the staircase, sneaking past each other's doors . . ."

"Some of us do that anyway," Meryl says, looking at Nick. He grins.

Aurora goes on. "I think this is going to be a really powerful production. I've already been able to make some very interesting choices."

"Why *did* you audition if you weren't sure?" I ask Nick.

"The fun of it."

Meryl blows air out of her cheeks. "So, wasting people's time is fun for you? Oh, wait, never mind, I already knew the answer to that."

Aurora says, "It's Nick's decision. I only want actors in my cast who'll be committed to the show."

"Of course. I just think—never mind. I have to get to work." Meryl gulps the last of her coffee and leaves.

I say, "I think you should do it."

Nick says, "I didn't say I wouldn't."

scene ii

"IT'S LOVELY TO see all of you," Aurora says. "Thanks for being prompt, which I'm sure you'll continue to be for all the upcoming rehearsals."

Something happens when Aurora walks into the theater. Even her voice is calm, focused, in charge.

"Today we'll be doing a read-through," she continues. "But first, I want to introduce Charles Fahey, our designer, and Robert Cracknell, who'll be building our set."

Charles smiles and hoists himself onto the stage. He's dressed up, sort of, in a charcoal Victorian frock suit with a hot pink tank top and matching high-top sneakers: half Dickensian street urchin, half cheerleader.

"Hi, everybody—I'm psyched about this show, but you know, because it's done so often, it's a real challenge to come up with a truly original vision, and I know we've all seen a lot of really bad, boring *Midsummer* designs in our lives."

We have?

"So I want to start by reassuring everyone that I'm not going to do cutesy twee fairies"—Charles flutters his hands at the word *twee*—"and I'm also not going to make everyone look like refugees from a Goth club. The goal, the overall look for the fairies, is simple but magical. There will be glitter, but there will not be bells."

Meryl leans over and whispers, "Thank fucking God. We had one show where *everyone's* costume had bells, and as soon as you went backstage, one of the stagehands had to throw a blanket over you to muffle the sound. It was hell."

"And as for Theseus's court," Charles continues, "we're going with simplicity there, too. Clean lines, but the palette will be a little dull, beige, like weathered Greek statues. And with the use of beige, I want it also to evoke bandages, because everything's contained and wrapped up in Athens; we also get a hint that way of how Theseus conquered Hippolyta in war. And we're going to use half masks to strengthen the sense of formality for the Athens scenes."

"Oh, please no masks! I *hate* masks, they make me break out!" Meryl says, loud enough for everyone to hear.

"*Half* masks, and they'll all be coming off when we leave Athens and get into the forest. The look in Athens needs to tell us the story of the court, which is all about people staying in their defined places. But then, since we've got the doubling with Theseus's court and the fairy court, the fairy costumes are also going to be sort of exploded, deconstructed versions of the look for the court."

"That sounds suspiciously like the RSC production of '99," the ogre shouts out.

"Who's he?" I whisper.

Meryl leans in very close. "That's Henry. He and Aurora used to have a *thing*." Her lips brush my ear, which makes it hard to concentrate, but I listen as she continues, "They don't anymore, obviously, but they're, like, super amicable exes now. *And* Henry's totally loaded. He puts up a lot of cash for the shows, so pretty much, he can do anything he wants. Thank God he can act."

This last sentence sounds loud, even though Meryl's still whispering, because Charles has finished talking about the costumes.

"Thanks, Charles," Aurora says. "Robert, before you tell us about the set, I want to talk a little about how I see the play."

The look she and Robert exchange makes me think they must have made up. Which clears up the question of what the sounds were the other night. Ew.

"When people say they want a traditional *Dream*, they mostly mean Victorian—masses of fairies; huge, lavish sets; lots of Mendelssohn—"

"What've you got against Mendelssohn?" Henry interrupts again.

"I have nothing at all, Henry, against Mendelssohn as a composer, but when he gets in the way of Shakespeare, I have a problem. And when people talk about an *edgy* interpretation—a word I loathe, by the way, please don't talk to me about anything being *edgy*—they mean that it's all about the sex. So the Victorian-style 'traditional,' the salacious 'edgy'—

neither is what we're after. Dismiss them from your minds."

They weren't *in* my mind.

"What I want us to create together is a *Dream* that's about the way the *forest* changes everyone who goes in. In the Middle Ages, not too long before Shakespeare's time, remember, the forest, outside the city walls, was where you'd find outlaws and madmen. And I want you all to be thinking about that idea of the forest, as a place of both opportunity and threat. And then there's the aspect of the *Dream as* dream—a state where anything can happen, and the only logic that operates is dream-logic."

Does Aurora teach? She sounds like a professor.

"And, of course, there's also just pure silliness, we can't forget that aspect, either—though we want to think about who's really laughing at whom, and keep that a little surprising.

"So, Robert, tell us about what we're going to be moving through in our *Dream*."

Robert stands up. "Okay. Well, physically, what you're going to be moving through is, uh, not a whole lot. Charles already mentioned that the basic idea we're working with is that the court and the wood are sort of versions of each other."

Charles interrupts. "The court is about hierarchies and repression and the wood is about everything turning inside out and reversing—"

Robert interrupts him in turn. "And that's what we're

going to do—build some Greek columns that'll reverse to abstract trees. That'll let us get from Athens into the forest real fast. And we're reinforcing the different settings mostly with painted curtains, and by the way, I could use everyone's help on those."

"I'm not quite grasping your overall concept," Henry says.

Robert laughs. "My concept is that our budget for sets is two hundred bucks. We're gonna do what we can."

Before the read-through, Aurora has us sit in a circle on the stage and introduce ourselves.

When I say my name, I get a bunch of double takes. I assume some of them are due to the name itself, which often surprises people, but then I add, "I'm Nick's sister, and I just moved here." This makes several people nod in that "*now* I get it" way, and look from me to him and back again. I wonder how many of the actors know him from other shows.

The black-haired, thick-necked boy playing Demetrius looks more like a quarterback than an actor. Lysander is a redhead, built like a gymnast. His shoulder-length hair is pulled back with a leather strap, and he does a split before settling into a cross-legged yoga pose. Show-off.

Oberon/Theseus is a short, bald black man; Titania/Hippolyta is a tall blonde. I remember both of their auditions. They were good. The other fairies—Moth, Peaseblossom, Mustardseed, and Cobweb—are all girls in middle school. I can already tell I'm going to have trouble telling them apart. They all fidget a lot, twirling their hair, filing their nails, pushing their bracelets on and off. They only stop fidgeting when Lysander, Demetrius, or Puck—Nick—is reading. Demetrius and Lysander don't seem to notice, but Nick does. Every so often he pauses during his reading and smiles at his fairy fan club.

Henry—the formerly seersucker-clad ogre, who's wearing a dazzlingly bright Hawaiian shirt and khakis today—is Bottom the weaver, the ham who wants every part in the play-within-a-play. It doesn't surprise me that Henry plays him completely over the top. But I like him, too. There are only a few people—Egeus, Lysander, Quince—whose readings seem off or bad to me, and that makes me impressed again with Aurora.

Soon it's time for the scene where Lysander and Demetrius both claim to love Helena instead of Hermia, and Helena decides that they're all three making fun of her. She's especially upset because she and Hermia have been friends for years, and she reproaches Hermia in a long speech.

I scoot closer to Meryl, looking up from the script as often as I can manage without losing my place.

"So we grew together, like to a double cherry—"

Lysander stifles a giggle, which sets off the middle-school fairies. Aurora freezes them all with a look, and I go on.

At the end of the read-through, Aurora says, "There's just one other thing I want to mention, so that you can—I hope—arrange your schedules so you're able to make it. I've reserved several spaces at a campground a couple of hours from here, for a few weekends from now. Since so much of the *Dream* is about what happens in the woods, I want as many of us as possible to spend some time in a real forest—and I'll want to run some scenes while we're there. Even though we won't be performing outdoors this time, it's good to get the experience of rehearsing outside."

"What if you don't have a tent?" one of the middle-school fairies asks.

"Then it's the dank and dirty ground for you, young lady," says Nick. The fairy giggles.

"I'm sure we'll be able to work something out," Aurora says. "Lots of people have tents."

AFTER REHEARSAL, NICK, Meryl, Aurora, Robert, and I stop to pick up some Lebanese food at a tiny, crowded, delicious-smelling restaurant. It's Aurora's night to cook, but apparently takeout is an acceptable and frequent alternative to actual food preparation. We get back to Forest House and find Charles at the dining-room table, shuffling a deck of cards. He's taken off his Victorian suitcoat, and I notice how thin and pale his arms are. He has a barbed-wire tattoo on his right forearm. He glares at us all.

"Thanks for waiting for me," he says to Nick.

"I didn't see you after, so I thought you'd left already. Where were you?"

"Where do you *think* I was? Where am I *always* during a show? Maybe, oh, I don't know, the *costume* shop?"

Aurora takes the sacks of food into the kitchen. Robert follows her. Meryl rummages in her bag for her cigarettes and heads for the back porch. It feels like I should go elsewhere, too, but something stops me.

Charles says, "I was expecting you. You said you'd meet me."

"Sorry, love," Nick says. "It slipped my mind. But hey, there's pita bread and hummus and tabbouleh and baba ghanoush and falafel."

Love?

Charles picks up a card, stares at it, puts it back in the deck. Then he looks up at Nick.

"I never see you anymore."

That makes two of us.

"Sure you do. You'll see me tonight."

Nick smiles in a way that makes me even more sure I shouldn't be here.

Charles shuffles again.

"Watch it, sweetheart, you're gonna wear out that deck," Nick says. He traces circles with one finger on the back of Charles's neck.

"Cards wear out," Charles says, and his voice has

changed—it's like *he's* the one onstage. "You should know that. And when they do, I'll just do what Frankie did. Frankie and Johnny were sweethearts—you know the song, right? You know it was real, it really happened. She ended up here after she killed him, because the other places she moved, the song followed her. She was going to become respectable, have a good life, right? So she'd sit in her living room and play solitaire, and whenever she wore out a deck, she'd rip open another one."

Charles deals himself another hand.

"Respectability sounds boring," Nick says. He peers at the cards. "You'd better reshuffle; you'll never win with that layout. Besides, there's three of us—we could play hearts!"

He still plays it, then.

"I'm tired of hearts. Eventually she went insane. And who says I want to win?"

I pick up a dead leaf from the floor, crumple it in my hand. I still can't manage to make myself leave the room.

"All right then," Nick says. "Have fun not winning. I'll see you later." He leans down and kisses Charles's neck. I shiver.

I have too many questions, so what I ask is, "Where are you going? Aren't you going to eat?"

"Work. I'll eat later. And speaking of work, you should be memorizing your lines, Helena. It's never too early."

"What about *your* lines?"

"Don't worry about me." He grins at us, then walks out.

Instead of pulling out my script, I watch Charles.

My brother's boyfriend, I guess.

Maybe it wasn't Robert and Aurora that I heard the other night.

Blech.

Not that I'm squicked by the idea of my brother having a boyfriend. If I were, I'd be a huge hypocrite.

I'm squicked by the idea of him having sex. With *anyone*.

Meanwhile, Charles plays the hand of solitaire fast, and wins.

"Someday," says Charles, as he gathers the cards for another hand, "he's going to do something he won't be able to get away with."

"What did you mean when you said 'the song followed her'?" I ask.

I only seem to be able to ask the wrong questions.

Charles doesn't look up from his shuffling. "She killed him in St. Louis, and everybody was singing about it as soon as the trial was over. So she moved to Omaha, but people were singing 'Frankie and Johnny' there, too. She came to Portland to get away, but it couldn't have been long before the song showed up. She couldn't ever escape from it, you see?"

"Yeah. I think so."

He begins to deal the cards again. I shift from foot to foot, watching him, then finally say, "You could come eat dinner. If you want."

Charles sighs, gathers the cards, and slides them back into their box. Then he nods and follows me into the kitchen.

scene iii

AFTER A BRIEF interval of cursing myself for not setting up a high-powered internship—ignoring, again, the fact that I have no idea where I'd want to intern—I find a part-time job that's posted on a Web site called Craigslist: canvassing for an environmental organization. I could've afforded—barely—to live off my savings, but I promised Mom and Dad that I'd find something, so I did. And they seemed pleased when I made my weekly call and told them.

My job: I stand on a street corner in a hippie shopping neighborhood and try to get people to sign a petition I'm not even sure *I* agree with.

Soon I find a coffeehouse I like near the Reed campus, and sometimes I sit there with my script and my laptop, alternating between learning lines and being online. Other days when I'm not working, I lose hours in the stacks of the downtown library. It has an art gallery on the top floor, and a huge chandelier and a marble staircase, and overall, it looks like a person would need to be formally dressed even to be allowed inside, let alone to check anything out.

At Forest House, I learn who does their dishes (Charles, Robert); who abandons them all over the house (Aurora, Meryl); who gets angry when you move their stuff, even if it's because you're cleaning (everyone); who always wants to talk, even when—or especially when—it's really late (Aurora, Meryl, Charles); and who doesn't actually seem to live in the house (my brother).

Nick's work schedule seems to be: as many hours in a row as possible, with occasional breaks for sleep. Every time I do see him, he's either on the way to his room to crash, or on his way out the door. The only place I know I'll see him is rehearsal. Then late Saturday morning, he turns up at the house with doughnuts and bagels for everyone, including a gluten- and dairy-free selection for Aurora, who apparently has complex and ever-shifting food issues, and vegetarian lox for Charles.

"How the hell do you make vegetarian *lox*?" Robert demands.

"I bet it's tofu with food coloring, like everything else vegetarian," says Meryl.

"It's delicious. Thank you," Charles says.

"And that's not all," Nick says. "I've also got *mail*! Mr.

Robert Cracknell, some fabulous low-interest credit card offers for you; Ms. Meryl Davenport, here's a postcard from illegible, hoping that you're unreadable; Ms. Aurora Kneedler, *Theatre Weekly*; and last but certainly not least, for Mr. Charles Fahey, a plain brown envelope. Nothing for you, Battle—sorry."

"I wasn't expecting anything."

Robert says, "Nick gave you the address for the P.O. box, right? We had some trouble in the past with mail disappearing. You know with identity theft, that's often what they do: steal the mail."

I nod, even though I don't quite know what he's talking about. Robert makes me nervous. He hasn't been hostile since the day I moved in, but I assume it's because he's written me off as a drunken reprobate.

When Nick gets up from the table, I ask, "Back to work?"

"Nah. My time is my own today."

"Take me with you," I say. I sound like I'm nine.

"You don't know where I'm going!"

"I know."

"What if I'm not going anywhere interesting?"

"I don't care. I never see you." Now I sound like Charles.

Nick's long-suffering sigh sounds just like it did when I'd try following him around when we were little.

"Never mind," I say.

And he walks out.

But a few hours later, after I've read all the comics someone left on the coffee table and am considering cracking open the script, which has been on the table next to them the entire time, he comes back.

He's got a big smile on his face. "Hey, slacker! Still want to get in some quality time? Get up, I'm gonna take you to a bona fide historical landmark. You get to drive."

I glance at the script, and Nick grabs it. "You can do that anytime. C'mon."

He leads me out to my car, opens the door for me like a gentleman, and directs me into a section of the city I haven't seen before: the southwest. Big trees, big houses.

"So this guy, Mr. Pittock—turn here—starts up a big news-paper. He does really well. So well that he decides to build a giant-ass house because, you know, he's rich, and that's what you do. He puts together plans for this ginormous place, lots of marble, lots of wood—they decorate the hell out of it for Christmas—superdeluxe furniture, a kitchen that's absolutely state-of-the-art for the time—there's an intercom, even. You won't believe it."

"Cool."

"Hey, the entrance is coming up. You see the sign?"

There's a large parking lot with just a few cars in it.

"It's a good time to come; it's not as packed as usual."

We get out of the car and begin walking up the path. Soon

the mansion comes into view through the trees. It looks like the set of one of those old English movies where everyone's gathered for a weekend house party and then someone gets murdered.

Inside the entrance hall, a gray-haired woman sits at a table with a cash box. I reach for my wallet, but Nick says, "No, no, your money's no good here. Allow me."

He pays our admissions and the woman smiles.

"Enjoy yourselves. The next tour starts in ten minutes."

"Thanks! I know we will," Nick says, smiling back.

It reminds me of a field trip. Our small, well-behaved group goes from room to lavishly furnished room. The guide tells us about the family, whose oversized portraits hang on one wall, and points out interesting features of the house's construction. I feel like I should be taking notes for a report.

"How many times have you come here?" I ask Nick when we're halfway up the wide central marble staircase.

"Imagine performing in this space," Nick says. "Can't you see this as the court of Theseus? So much excess and wealth. And the property's vast—you could do the forest scenes outdoors, get the audience to follow you out . . ."

"Would Aurora do that?"

"She might. It's hard to say. Sometimes she surprises you. Oh, hey, there's a fantastic view. Go on, check it out."

Nick points to a set of French doors that lead onto a balcony. I go out, and he's right. I can see the whole city.

"Excuse me, miss?" A guide is next to me. "I'm sorry, but we can't allow anyone outside, it's too great a risk, liability-wise. I certainly regret it, because it's a lovely view, isn't it? But we need to go back inside now."

"I apologize. My brother . . ." I look for Nick, and see, out of the corner of my eye, that he's slipping something small and green from a desk into a pocket of his baggy shorts.

"Sorry?"

"Nothing, sorry," I say, noting that we've now apologized to each other twice.

Nick, when I find him, is examining a set of skis in a glass case, from a polite distance.

"It's not allowed, going outside," I say.

"Really? They must've changed the policy since the last time I was here. Did they hassle you? Do I need to bust some heads? Man, can you believe this place? I love it, it's so over the top, but sometimes I just have to laugh. I mean, here, for example, is a perfectly good pair of skis. Somebody could be using them and instead they're behind glass like medieval relics. Hey, do you think they have special powers? Like if you touch them, you'll suddenly get really good at skiing?"

"I don't think you should *touch* anything else here."

He keeps looking at the skis. "It's like flying, but you're always headed downhill."

"Those are cross-country skis. You can go anywhere you want."

I see that the guide who told me about the balcony being off-limits is talking to another guide.

Now she's pointing at us.

I nudge Nick. Guiltily.

Like it's my fault.

The two guides start walking toward us.

"Excuse me," one of them says.

Could you please turn out your pockets.

The police are on their way.

We're going to place you both under arrest.

Nick takes me by the arm and steers us toward the stair-case.

"Excuse me." Louder.

We start down the stairs.

"Excuse me!"

I stop, frozen. Nick pulls on my arm, but I don't move.

I'm sure it'll be worse if we run away and they have to chase us down.

What the fuck was it that he took?

Morality aside, whatever it was, it's not worth going to jail for.

"Excuse me!"

This is it, then. I turn and face the angry guides.

"Yes?"

The first guide thrusts a slip of paper at me. "If you're not going to keep your receipt, we *have* wastebaskets. We're a volunteer operation here. We don't have staff to go around picking up after people."

Nick shakes his head and says, "I can't take you anywhere."

Now I want either to crack up or hit my brother.

"I'm so sorry, it must've slipped out," I say, showing the guides the wide gap of my hoodie's central pocket. "I'll take it now."

I hold on to the little piece of paper as though it's a hundred-dollar bill. The guides sniff, nod, and go away.

I open my mouth and before I can get a word out, Nick asks, "Had enough? We can take off, then. But did you get the whole story of the place?"

"No," I say very quietly. "I got a little distracted while you were stealing."

"What?"

"You heard me."

"I have no idea what you're talking about. Okay, so the guy started *planning* this place when he was already in his seventies. By the time it was finally done, he and his wife only lived here for, like, four years. Because they were old! They died!"

We're walking past the ticket-taker when Nick says this,

61

and he flashes her another smile. This time she doesn't smile back.

"I think that's sad," I say.

"Of course it's sad! That's why it's so perfect. You know, it's a monument to the futility of human ambition. Look on my works, ye mighty, and despair."

I look back at the mansion. Have they noticed yet that something small and green is missing?

Or did I imagine it?

"I thought you liked the place. I mean, the architecture and the furniture and everything."

"I do! It's fantastic! But it's the story that makes it."

Our "quality time" continues with a stop for coffee—I think I've had more coffee since I've been in Portland than in my entire previous life, even counting midterms, finals, and the cross-country drive—and then we go back to Forest House. The whole time, Nick's telling me this long, convoluted story about some friend of his and the ridiculous, horrible things that have happened to him.

He doesn't seem to notice my silence. After I retrieve my script from the coffee table, Nick follows me up to my room, turns on my computer, and goes to some game site I haven't seen before. Like it belongs to him. I'm opening my mouth to say something—what, I don't know—when I hear my phone play the opening of Beethoven's Fifth Symphony.

It's the ring for my parents.

Our parents.

Fuck. The mansion people found out what Nick stole and notified Mom and Dad.

No. The mansion people have no way of knowing who he is.

And Mom and Dad don't know I'm living with him.

I've just forgotten to make my weekly call.

I pick up on the fifth ring.

"Hello?" As though I don't know who it is.

"Busy week?" Dad asks. His voice is so loud, I'm sure Nick can hear.

I see his back stiffen.

"Yeah, it has been. I'm sorry I haven't talked to y'all—I've been running around a lot the last few days."

"We miss you!" Mom says.

"I miss y'all, too."

"Gee whiz," says Nick, "I sure do miss our special family times."

I walk over to where he's sitting and mouth "Shut up."

"How's that job going?" Dad asks.

This is the first summer I can remember that I haven't been at camp, taking classes, or both.

"It's fine. And I'm getting to know the city. It's beautiful here. I'm really grateful to have the chance to get my bearings a little before school starts."

"Ever indebted to my beloved parents, eager to do all they

should ever require of me!" Nick says heartily, with an English accent.

"Is there someone else with you, dear?" Mom asks. "It sounds like a boy!"

"It's just the TV." I make throat-cutting gestures at Nick.

I don't know which irritates me more, what he's doing or how pleased Mom seems to be at me having a boy in my room.

Nick starts humming a theme song.

I open a window on the computer screen and type: WANT ME TO PUT YOU ON??? THEY'D LOVE IT.

"It's a lot of responsibility," Dad says. He said the same thing a number of times before I left.

Nick types: NO.

"I know," I say. To both of them.

"We're trusting you to be smart about the way you spend your time," Mom says.

"And who you spend it with," Dad adds.

"I've barely even met anyone. I probably won't make any friends until I get on campus."

It's so easy to keep lying.

Is this what Nick feels like all the time?

"Regardless. I hope you know how important it is for you to be careful. And you'd better be watching your budget. There aren't many people your age who are in charge of their own college money. We are placing a great deal of trust in you, young lady."

"And I pray to God that trust is not misplaced," Nick says, this time in a very good imitation of Dad's voice.

SHUT THE FUCK UP, I type. OR I SWEAR I'LL TELL THEM RIGHT NOW.

Nick laughs. But then he closes the Web browser and leaves the room.

"I know," I say.

I tell them more about the canvassing job, and they're glad I've found one, though Mom is a little concerned because it consists almost entirely of talking to strangers.

She updates me on the social lives of various members of Dad's congregation. Dad says that the new youth minister's shaking things up some. I make interested-sounding noises. Eventually we all run out of things to say.

scene iv

THE NEXT DAY, the first thing I notice when I wake up is that I've managed to snag my right thumbnail. I raise my thumb to my mouth to bite off the snag, then stop myself.

I find Meryl on the back porch, smoking and muttering.

"By all the vows that ever men have broke, in number more than ever women spoke . . . Oh, hi."

I smile. "Hi."

We stare out at the back garden. All the flowers are white. I didn't know there were so many different kinds of white flowers.

"How does Aurora have time to *do* all this?"

"She doesn't. It's Charles."

"Oh, right. He told me that. Still. Wow."

"He's nuts about gardening. It works like meds for him: calming, stabilizing. Design does, too. If he's sewing or digging in the dirt, our Charles is happy."

"*Should* he be on meds?" With the possible exception of Robert, Charles seems like the most stable person in Forest House.

"I try not to judge other people," Meryl says.

I curl my thumb into my palm. "Okay—then may I ask you a weird question?"

"Sure."

"Where would you go around here to get a manicure?"

Meryl glances at her own small, short-nailed hands, then at mine.

"I'm not really a big manicure getter. Aurora would probably have a better idea."

"But you know the city, and I need to get it soon. Like, today. This morning, if possible."

"Why?"

I hold up my thumb. "Slippery slope."

"I still don't get it."

I wiggle the snagged nail back and forth, then bury my thumb in my palm again, closing my fingers around it.

"If I don't get a manicure, I'll rip this nail off. It will bleed. Then I'll start going after my cuticles. Within the hour, I'll have at least six open wounds."

"Some people just clip their nails," Meryl says. She digs in her pocket and pulls out a pair of clippers attached to a key chain.

"In that case, I cut them all down to the quick, and cut off some skin while I'm at it, so it ends up the same."

Meryl rolls her eyes. "Give me your hand."

Her hands might as well be jumper cables. Now I wish all my nails were snagged.

"There," she says, clipping. "All better." She lets go.

I force myself to focus on my hand. "There's still some cuticles that are just about ready to tear."

"I guess I should take you to a manicure place, then, huh?"

"Would you?"

Meryl grins. "Sure, but I'm starved. Let's go to breakfast first."

"Okay." This is the first one-on-one time I've spent with her since the day I arrived.

It feels like suddenly none of my clothes fit properly. I pluck at my T-shirt, shove my hands into the pockets of my jeans, realize I've been standing in fifth position, shift to first.

"I'm gonna take you to my favorite place. It's so awesome," Meryl says. "The coffee's self-serve, and you can keep getting refills until your eyes roll back into your head."

When we're there, seated outside in a little courtyard, the waitress says to Meryl, "Every time you come in here, you're with someone new—what's your secret?"

Meryl blushes. "Shut up. God."

The waitress says to me, "You watch her. So what can I get for the two of you today?"

Oatmeal and fruit for me, biscuits and gravy for Meryl. The waitress walks away, stepping aside to avoid a golden retriever puppy who's straining at his leash to reach a dropped piece of bacon. There are several dogs in the courtyard, which makes me like the restaurant already.

Meryl says, "One thing you'll learn—Portland may seem like a big city at first, but really, it's a very small town."

"So, who *were* you with the last time you were here?"

"God, I don't even know," she says, lighting a cigarette. "I come here all the time; I drag all kinds of people in. I love the food." She exhales casually. "It might even have been your brother."

"Hmm." I sip my coffee.

"Don't take this the wrong way, but you kind of don't seem like the *type* to get your nails done," Meryl says.

Just what *type* does she think I am?

She goes on, "You had a premanicure era, right? So . . . what happened?"

"My mom. She hated seeing my hands when my nails were all ripped up. One day she just took me to a salon."

"Huh," Meryl says. "I doubt my mom would notice if I was missing an entire finger. Your mom must be cool."

I don't know what to say, so I say nothing. "Cool" is just about the last word I'd choose to describe Mom.

Meryl shrugs. "Anyway, I think those manicure places are creepy. Isn't it weird to have somebody do your personal grooming for you?"

I'm watching the puppy. He still can't reach the bacon. Someone throws him a piece of biscuit and he gulps it. "Eh, it keeps me from messing myself up," I say. "My hands, anyway."

"It must be super expensive. I wouldn't be able to afford it."

"Not really. Besides, you could spend less money on something else. Like cigarettes." Some of her smoke reaches me, and I plug my nose, the way I used to do with my friend Katrina when she insisted on smoking around me.

It never worked on her, either.

Meryl laughs. "We're outside! You're not breathing in any more poison than you'd get if you were riding your bike behind an SUV."

"Another activity I really enjoy seeking out."

Meryl waves her hand dismissively.

"So," she says, "how do you like Portland?"

"Fine."

"It must be hard—I mean, you moved so far." Meryl leans in close. "Who was it hardest to leave behind?"

I shrug.

"Come on. Who were you closest to? You know, you say you're going to stay important to each other, but somehow when you're not in the same place anymore, it's just hard, and you each have your own life, and there's still something there you don't want to lose, but you can't figure out how to reach it?"

I don't know how to respond to this, either. It's such a personal question, but somehow it doesn't quite feel like Meryl asked it because she's interested in *me*. It's more like she wants to extract a story, and I find that I don't want her to take it from me.

So I look away, without saying anything.

Even now, every time I see a girl with long brown hair I do a double take. But, of course, it's never Nicola Lancaster.

Finally, because Meryl won't stop looking at me, I laugh a

little, shake my head, and say, "There was no one special in Chapel Hill."

"So, from somewhere else, right?"

I will myself not to change expression.

"I can always tell," Meryl says. "There's something about you . . . it's like you hold back part of yourself—you don't want to put it all out there."

I'm furious. "Why don't you guess my star sign, too? Want to read my palm? Or go through my wallet?"

"I don't need to see your wallet. You're a Virgo."

And as a matter of fact, I am.

THE SALON MERYL finds is large, stark white, and clinical, with several manicure tables and a few pedicure stations that look like high-tech black vinyl thrones. All these are occupied by young Vietnamese men watching football on a big-screen TV while women—also Vietnamese—work on their feet.

"You know I've never done this before," Meryl says.

"Well, it's important to seek out new experiences."

"There's something you can get where you hardly look like you have nail polish on at all, but your hands look clean. It masks the dirt under your nails. What's that called?"

"A French manicure."

"Why is that French? What's French about it?"

"I have no idea, but it's what I always get. Just tell them that's what you want."

AN HOUR LATER, we leave with matching French manicures. Meryl can't stop staring at her hands. "Are you sure the polish is dry? This is *so* weird. And that part where they pick your cuticles *for* you? It's bizarre. Where did this practice originate? How long have chicks been doing this?"

"You say that like you're not a chick," I say, amused.

"I'm not. I'm more of a babe. Now we have to do something *you've* never done before."

"Okay." This sounds much better than her trying to interrogate me about my life. "What do you think I haven't done?"

Meryl eyes me appraisingly. "I could guess some things, but I won't. You might surprise me."

"Then how will you know if you're right?"

Meryl smiles. "I'll know."

Meryl's truck is both loud and wheezy, like a consumptive's cough. It makes it hard to talk, but I like the silence. While Meryl watches the road, I watch her. She drives fast. There's something about her expression, her focused attention to the traffic, that reminds me of Nic.

So stupid that my brother and my first girlfriend have the same name.

First. As though there've been others.

As though it was conceivable to think about having a girl-friend while living under my parents' roof. Last year, shortly after the Head-Shaving Fallout, we had The Conversation About The Gay. To say the least, Mom and Dad weren't thrilled to learn that I like girls, you know, *that way.* Mom kept talking about how she was afraid my life would be so hard, "living that lifestyle."

Like life is so much easier if you just pretend to be someone you're not. But at the end of it, I didn't get disowned or kicked out of the house.

Maybe because they were estranged from one kid already.

I inch my hand across the seat toward Meryl's leg.

"We've got to stop here first," she says, pulling over at a roadside produce stand. "Can you see, do they have canta-loupe?"

"I hate to tell you this, but I've eaten cantaloupe before."

"That's not what I need it for."

What else do you do with cantaloupe?

My thoughts go X-rated.

"There's some other kinds of melon," I say, carefully neutral. "Will any of them work?"

Meryl frowns. "I always use a cantaloupe."

"Um. Should I ask?"

"No. Stay in the car, I'll be right back."

In a few minutes, Meryl returns holding a melon. She raps the side and it makes a hollow but satisfying sound.

"Crenshaw," she says. "They have a harder shell, but that'll be better, come to think of it. Hold it till we get there, okay?"

"Sure." I put it on my lap. The scent of the fruit fills the car—sweet, but not cloying.

I read the label out loud: "'When fully ripe, a Crenshaw will be fragrant and yield slightly to gentle pressure at its blossom end.' Which is the blossom end, do you think?"

Meryl reaches over and runs her hands over the rind, not taking her eyes off the road. "Here, where the stem is, probably. It doesn't matter, though, for what we'll be doing."

"Which is?"

"I might be wrong, by the way," Meryl says. "You may have done it a million times. Considering where you grew up, especially. But you and Nick—neither of you seem super Southern."

"What would super Southern be like?"

"Oh, you know, a lot more drawl, for starters."

"Why is it always about the accent?"

Meryl makes a sharp left, sharp enough that I slide across the seat and our legs touch.

"Hey, sorry about that, I always almost miss this turn."

"No problem," I say, not moving back. "Go on about what super Southern is like."

"Oh, right. Well, you don't tell stories. Nick does—in

a way—but you don't, and I think of that as being a big Southern thing."

"Just because you haven't heard any is no reason to conclude that I don't."

I spin the melon in my hands like a basketball.

I'm flirting. Is she?

"So how long do you have to know someone before you start telling your stories?"

She is.

"That depends on the person."

"Damn," Meryl says. "Not about your stories. I'm an idiot. We can't take the melon in. But it's okay, because we can still eat it, later. And we'll still go, yeah. Okay, I'll have to explain. It won't be as . . . graphic, but. So. That melon you've got in your hands. Pretty hard rind, right? I'm going to ask you to imagine two things, one after the other. Can I trust that you have a vivid imagination?"

Getting more vivid by the minute. "Yes."

"Good. What would happen if a bullet hit that melon?"

I look at Meryl, then at the melon. "It would explode?"

"And what would that look like?"

"Well, it would fly out of my hands, and there'd be pieces of rind, and seeds, and . . . what do you call the part you eat?"

"The flesh," Meryl says. "Good. Imagine that it was your head."

Now the X rating is for horror.

"Why?"

"I'm taking you to a gun range. Ever fired a gun?"

"No."

"Ha! I knew it! That was how I got my first gun safety lesson. Dad set a cantaloupe on a fence post in our backyard and then he blew it away with his shotgun—no warning, nothing."

"Dang. How big is your yard? And how old were you?"

Meryl laughs. "The yard is big. The *trailer* is small, but we have a lot of land. I was five. Maybe six. He told me to think about if it had been my head. Or his. And that I should respect guns, always assume they're loaded, always be super careful around them. But the place we're going, it's an indoor range, so we can only shoot paper targets, we can't take out any fruit. What was I thinking? Must be something toxic in this *nail polish*, messing up my brain chemistry."

"Do you shoot a lot?" It's not something I would've pictured. But then, there's a lot about her I wouldn't have pictured.

"I like to, yeah. It can get expensive, though. You're up for kicking in some cash for a new experience, right?"

"Sure."

"Good. That's a nice change."

From what?

Meryl pulls up outside a long, low gray building, with a few cars and several trucks parked outside. I'm about to open my door when she puts a hand on my thigh.

"Wait. I didn't ask—are you nervous?"

I stare at the contrast between the white-painted tips of Meryl's fingernails and the dark blue of my jeans, feel the pressure of Meryl's small hand, hyperaware that there's only one layer of fabric between it and my skin.

"Yes."

"Good. If you weren't, I'd be worried."

INSIDE, A PRETTY woman is standing behind a big glass display case that contains a dozen or so guns of assorted sizes, carefully labeled. I know from movies and TV that the numbers refer to the type of bullets the gun shoots, but the manufacturer's names and the accompanying descriptions mean nothing.

On the wall behind the woman hangs a display of all the paper targets available for sale. Bull's-eyes, silhouettes, bottles and cans on a fence. Exaggerated cartoonish portraits designed to resemble Bad Guys, and a couple of Bad Girls, too. I'm not sure whether or not to be pleased at this evidence of ballistic equal opportunity. All the Bad People targets are snarling and holding guns. The creepiest one is a Bad Guy holding a gun to a panicked woman's head.

The range itself is visible through a bank of windows. It's

divided into lanes, like a potentially lethal bowling alley. Through the glass I can see men and women shooting at targets. Some are by themselves, some are in couples.

What a weird date.

Are we on one, too?

"Hi there!" the woman says. "What can I do for you two?"

"We need a .22, semiautomatic, and, let's see, I guess a couple of boxes of shells," Meryl says.

"Great—did you bring your own protection?"

"No."

"Okay, so you're gonna need two ears and two eyes."

The woman retrieves two pairs of earmuffs and two sets of safety glasses from bins behind the counter.

"You're going to need to keep these on the whole time you're shooting," she says to me. "And believe me, once you're inside there"—she gestures over to the range—"you will have *no* interest in taking them off!" She laughs.

Meryl says, "Seriously. Gun ranges are like the loudest places on the planet."

The woman gets a small gun from the second shelf of the display case and sets it on the counter, the barrel facing away from us. Then, as far as I can tell, she takes the gun apart. "That's the clip," Meryl tells me, touching the part the woman's just removed. "That's where you load the bullets." Then, to the woman, "This is her first time shooting."

"Oh, great!" says the woman. She addresses me: "And you always, always check to make sure it's unloaded."

"May I take a closer look at it before we decide?" Meryl asks.

The woman nods.

Meryl picks up the gun carefully, keeping it pointed at the floor. She takes out the clip, puts it in again, nods. "I think this one will work fine."

"Great! I'll show you how to load it."

It reminds me a little of putting staples into a stapler. You slide each bullet into the clip, and the bullets are shaped so they'll only fit one way: the right way. It's easy.

Scarily easy.

Meryl rests her hand on my shoulder. "Okay, lady, you get to pick the target."

I don't want to shoot anything that looks like a person.

"The bottles and cans, maybe?"

The woman says, "That's a hard one! Sure!" She lifts the target off the wall and hands it to me.

"So here's something else," Meryl says. "When you shoot, where do you think you're going to be looking?"

It seems obvious. "At the target?"

Meryl shakes her head. "You're going to look through the sight. Let me show you. Have you got a piece of paper I could use?" she asks. The woman nods, gives Meryl a blank receipt.

Meryl draws a **U**, and then a vertical line coming up from the middle of the **U**. "You want to look at the target first, then line it up in the sight, which is on top of the gun. It looks kind of like what I just drew, see?" She shows me the sight on our gun. "It doesn't work as well when you look right at what you're trying to hit."

"Okay."

Before we can go into the range, we each have to sign a form.

I read it out loud, like I did with the melon's label: "'I agree that I will be responsible for any damages that occur as a result of my careless actions.'"

Meryl says, "Don't you wish people had to sign that for real life?"

I laugh and nod.

I carry the target. Meryl has the gun and two boxes of shells in a plastic bucket. Like we're going to the beach to build sandcastles.

There's a woman and a man who may or may not be her husband in the lane next to us. They're smiling at each other as they trade off. She's a much better shot, and he doesn't seem to mind.

One man is by himself, firing round after round into the target with the picture of the Bad Guy with the gun to the woman's head. If it were real, the woman and her assailant would both be dead.

I can feel the vibrations when other people are shooting.

When we get to our lane, I yell, "You first!"

I try to pay attention to Meryl's careful stance, but when she raises her hands to shoot, her shirt rides up, letting me see an inch or so of smooth skin.

Then a spent shell bounces off my earmuffs, and I jump.

When it's my turn to take the gun, I have no idea how to hold it, and it's hard to focus on anything but the strength in Meryl's hands when she corrects my grip.

Pulling the trigger is a rush. I have no idea where my bullet went, though, except that it sure didn't make it into the target.

Meryl hits several of the bottles and cans. I hit one, I think, and a knothole in the fence the bottles and cans are on. But both those shots were nothing but luck.

Sooner than I would have thought, we run out of bullets.

"Want to get some more?" Meryl asks. I sort of want to, but my hands are tired and my ears are ringing, so I shake my head.

On our way out, we pass a sign that reads, REMEMBER, WHEN YOU WALK OUT OF HERE, THAT YOU REPRESENT ALL GUN ENTHUSIASTS. ACT ACCORDINGLY.

"So, d'you think I'm a crazy gun nut?" Meryl asks. We climb into the truck.

"No," I say.

"Was it like you thought it would be?"

Meryl buckles her seat belt and puts the key into the ignition, but for some reason, she doesn't start the engine right away.

"I had no idea what it'd be like. What did you think a manicure was going to be like?"

Meryl laughs. "Touché. See, that's why I like you. You surprise me."

I smile, then go slightly insane, deciding to do just that.

I lean over and kiss her.

Taste of tobacco and mint. Her tongue moving against mine, almost like she's fighting me. I cup my hand around the back of her neck, slide closer, and put my other arm around her, stroking the skin between her shirt and jeans with my other hand. I move my hand up her back, far enough to discover that she's not wearing a bra, and she gasps, breaks the kiss, and moves away.

We're both breathing hard.

"Wow," Meryl says. "Whew! I am *flattered*. Was it the shooting? It affects some people that way."

Meryl pats me on the knee, as though I'm a small child or a dog. She turns the key and the engine sputters into life.

This isn't how it's supposed to work.

Nic was always so willing to follow my lead, even though half the time I had no idea what I was doing.

I pick up the melon.

Then I crank the window down and throw it onto the road.

It explodes.

"Oops," I say.

"Goddammit, what'd you do that for? Look, I told you, I'm flattered, but it's a *rule* of mine not to get involved with housemates. And we're both in the show, and I'm older than you, and, you know, just, thanks but no thanks. But don't be mad. I had a good time today. I hope you did, too."

ACT III

It's a Trick-Taking Game

scene i

IT'S INDEPENDENCE DAY. I'd like to declare my independence from Forest House, but instead, I'm in the kitchen with Nick. So far, he's gotten out five bowls, three saucepans, the flour, the olive oil, every spice in the spice rack, and four packages of tempeh, but he hasn't yet made any effort to combine them.

"Of course it'll work," he says. "Cover *anything* in batter and fry it, and you're golden. I just can't quite bring the seasoning blend to mind."

He's making Mom's fried chicken, without the chicken.

"Don't you know the recipe?" he asks me. "I know there's paprika, and garlic . . . but what else?"

Meryl walks in from the back porch. "Oh, boy, I'd forgotten, it's not just a holiday, it's another Nick Davies culinary extravaganza. I can hardly wait, but I know I'm going to. Let's see, did we sit down at eleven the last time you cooked, or was it midnight?"

Nick smiles. "There weren't any leftovers."

She snorts.

"In fact, as I recall there were *several* factors contributing to the lateness of that particular meal. Cast your mind back." He smiles again.

Meryl blushes.

Then she says, "Whatever. I'm going out for some more appetite-suppressing nicotine."

"What was that about?" I'm not sure I want to know.

"Celery salt? Maybe a little sage?" Nick holds up the spices in question and contemplates them.

I shouldn't have worried.

"Why don't you just call Mom and ask?"

"You know that's not a good idea."

"Why not?"

He laughs. "'Cause you just talked to them the other day. You don't want to set their expectations too high."

"No, I said why don't *you* call?"

He doesn't seem to have heard me.

I go to my room to study my lines.

*　　*　　*

WHATEVER NICK ENDED up doing worked. Everyone liked the Southern-fried tempeh, even Robert.

Now we're all on the porch, and Nick's weighed down underneath a dozen boxes with labels like MAMMOTH SMOKE, PYROTECHNIC MOTHERLODE, and ARTIFICIAL SATELLITE.

"The only fireworks worth having are the kind where you might lose a finger," Nick says, "and they're only available from Nevada, the great state where games of chance and prostitution are valued as they should be everywhere in our nation."

Meryl flicks her lighter in his direction. "Careful."

"I'm the one who should be telling *you* that."

"I'm not the one holding the explosives."

"Oh, Nicholas, these look lovely! Every year I've been in this house, the displays have been truly extraordinary," Aurora said. She pours herself a glass of whiskey from the bottle she's holding. "I look forward to the Fourth of July more than any other holiday. Except Halloween."

"You've got to prepare yourself, okay?" Meryl hands me a plastic box full of wax earplugs. "Tonight is gonna make the gun range seem like—I don't know, like someplace where people are really quiet. I mean, every year it's like a fucking war zone on our block. I don't want you to lose your hearing."

"Thanks," I say, not meeting her eyes.

Kindness sucks.

It's like getting vanilla pudding when you want bananas Foster.

Nick's phone rings, and he sets the stack of boxes down to answer.

"Hello? What? Of *course*. Are you kidding? Absolutely. *Yes*. Why are you so agitated? Calm down. I am *going* to be there. I *know*. I am aware of that. Yes. Good-bye." He snaps the phone shut, shakes his head.

"I loathe fireworks," Charles says. "I wish I could get away, but there's no escape from them anywhere. Headphones help, but not enough. If I turn the volume up loud enough to drown them out, it's just another way to go deaf. I *wish* you wouldn't buy them."

"Who said I bought them?" Nick grins. I think again about the small green object from the mansion.

If I really saw what I thought I saw.

Robert clumps down the stairs and into the front yard with a pail of water in each hand. "Okay," he says, "you've got to make sure to have these close by, wherever you plan to set up."

Nick smiles at Robert. "You'd think you didn't trust me."

Robert just looks at him.

"Oh, Robert, you're so prudent," Aurora says. "You keep us all in line; it's so important." She lifts the glass to her lips.

"That's right. Robert's so prudent. He keeps us in line," Nick says.

It sounded like a compliment when Aurora said it.

"How about you?" Nick turns to me. "Are you prudent, or are you a pyro? There are only two choices."

"There are always more than two choices," Meryl says, shaking a cigarette out of a crumpled pack. "It's just that some people can only *see* two."

Nick points to Meryl's lighter. "Actions speak louder, pyro. Come on, Battle, tell our studio audience."

Just then, across the street, there's a squeal, a shower of sparks, and some applause.

"God, it's not even *dusk* yet. I'm going inside," Charles says, putting on his headphones.

I take the top box—INVASION FORCE ASSAULT—from the pile. Then I turn to Meryl. "May I borrow your lighter?"

A huge boom, then a red star bursts in the sky, then fades, then bursts again, larger, in blue.

"I hope you got some like that—they're my favorite," Meryl says. "When you're sure it's all over—then just when you least expect it, it goes off again."

"Okay, you're ready for launch," Nick says. "Light that fuse, then get away!"

I didn't put in the earplugs Meryl gave me, so it's even more of a shock than I expected, a shriek and then a bang, and just like Meryl said, it's even louder than the gun range. I almost forget to look up and see what I've set off: a cascade of white stars, then green, then a parachute that drifts down until it snags on a branch. Pretty gentle for an Invasion Force Assault.

Meryl and Nick and I take turns. Aurora applauds from the porch, drinking a toast to every launch, and Robert watches with his arms crossed, so clearly anticipating disaster that it's almost funny. Nick looks like—well, like Puck, or maybe Peter Pan, a feral boy delighted to be the cause of so much noise and light. Meryl's just like she was at the gun range—businesslike, professional.

I have no idea how I am.

Just as Nick's launching the Pyrotechnic Extravaganza, his phone rings again. He listens to the caller; he nods. "Great! Be right there."

The Extravaganza is a huge, lingering example of Meryl's favorite kind of firework, detonating in every color of the rainbow, but with pauses between each one that make you think it's over, until it begins again.

Nick snaps the phone shut and says, "You guys keep going, I've got to go to work. Have fun!"

He pushes open the fence and walks away, not looking back.

I decide to follow him.

We drive into a run-down neighboorhood.

I have to swerve periodically to avoid laughing groups setting off Roman candles and M-80s. A man and his dog are watching from the roof of a corner house. The explosions are nearly constant now, quick crackles, whistles, and one boom followed by a scream that makes me wonder if someone's chosen tonight to shoot their cheating spouse, under cover of all the other fire. I lock my doors, even though that makes me feel like an idiot, like I'm afraid someone's going to wrench open my door, jump inside, and menace me. Yeah, right, what a moron . . . oh wait, Nick's parking—shit, what for? I need to park, too. Now he's getting out. Where'd he go? Oh, into that gray building at the end of the block. But why? Isn't he just supposed to honk? Then another BOOM—much louder than any of the fireworks—and the car shakes and the steering wheel shifts in my hands.

"Dammit!"

I pull over. One of the front tires has blown; I must've driven over something. I scan the street and spot a broken bottle. From tonight, or left over from some other celebration, like breakfast?

If you drive on a flat, it messes up the car's alignment. Maybe Nick'll come out of the apartment and help me change it.

Right.

When I open the trunk, I see the scratches from when we got the furniture off the street.

Souvenirs.

"Hey!" A male voice. Not Nick's. It belongs to a tall guy wearing a Blazers jersey and long, baggy shorts. He's smoking something. "You all right?"

"Fine, thanks. This tire isn't, though."

The guy glances from my flat tire to the street.

"Goddamn. Hold up a second, I'll be right back."

He goes inside, comes out with a broom and a dustpan.

"Help me sweep that up, then we'll deal with the car."

He hands me the dustpan and we spend the next several minutes getting all the glass off the street. I can't help flinching each time another round goes off, and the air is thick with smoke and a burned-powder smell.

"Can't believe that mess. Some people're just ignorant," the guy says. "All right, let's get your tire changed."

Nick comes out, from a different apartment than either of the ones where I'd thought he was—and sees me.

"What the hell are you doing here?"

The guy says, "She's got a flat tire. You know her?"

"That's my brother," I say. The guy's expression shifts from friendly to cautious. Then he turns to Nick. "You wanna help me get this tire changed?"

"I can help you," I say.

"Thanks a lot," Nick says to the guy, all charm. "You know what? I think we're good. You should get back to the game, we can cope with it."

The guy looks from me to Nick and back again. Then he nods, and says to me, "All right. You come and knock on my door if you need anything. Four-oh-one."

Nick nods. I say, "I really appreciate your help."

The guy smiles at me, nods at Nick, goes back to his apartment.

Nick says, "You're leaving."

"I have to change the tire first."

"No, you don't. Get in the car."

"He was going to help me."

"You need to go."

"No," I say. "I'm not leaving the car here, and I'm not driving on a flat. I'm going to change it whether you help me or not."

"Why did you follow me?"

I lift the spare tire out of the trunk, then remember I should loosen the old tire first. So I hand the spare to Nick, then grab the jack, the torque wrench, and the set of lug wrenches Dad made me buy.

"Why did you *follow* me?"

I squat next to the tire. It's getting darker.

"There's a flashlight in the trunk. Hold it, so I can see what I'm doing."

He sighs, but then rummages in the trunk, finds the flashlight, shines it at the tire.

I position the jack, then start loosening the nuts holding the flat on.

Nick pushes at my arm. "Out of the way, let me do this."

I don't move. More booms.

Nick's flashlight shakes a little. "Hurry up, then."

"Why? Oh, that's right, I forgot, you were going to *work*!" I say, getting the wrench onto the first lug.

A truck screeches its brakes, then swerves around us.

"So are you *late* for work now?"

"Jesus, you're slow. That's going to take you forever."

I glare—not that Nick can see, since I'm glaring at the tire—and loosen each lug a half turn. It takes about five minutes. Then I jack up the car several inches. It's much easier than when I practiced it in Mom and Dad's driveway.

Adrenaline must help with upper-body strength.

All this time the fireworks keep exploding—every time there's a momentary pause, we relax, but then more go off, Nick's hands shake again, and I tense up. Every explosion is accompanied by shrieks, laughter, and applause. In between the fireworks, the pale shallow circle from the flashlight is the only illumination. All the streetlamps are burned out.

"So I'm a little confused," I say as I work, "about how this fits in with your job description."

"I'm a little confused about why you were following me."

"So what's going on? What are you *doing* here?"

"Why do you need to know?"

We're falling into an old pattern: alternating questions, neither of us giving or getting answers. It isn't conversation, and it isn't quite an argument. I don't know what it is, besides frustrating.

When I'm almost done, Blazers-jersey guy comes back.

"Are you in or out?" he asks Nick.

"In. It'll just be another minute."

"Of what?" I ask. Neither of them answers.

I tighten the last lug.

"Okay, you're all set," Nick says. "Now go home and celebrate freedom, all right?"

"What are *you* celebrating?"

"Go."

So I do, but I don't go back to Forest House. I sit in my favorite coffeehouse and brood. Between fireworks, I listen to one fussy young man teach another to play chess. He's a slow learner.

I think I am, too.

Hours later I'm still sitting there, so caffeinated that my hands are shaking, when my phone rings.

"Hey," Nick says, his voice warm and contented. "Come meet me. I'll buy you dinner." He gives me the address for a twenty-four-hour restaurant.

After a silence long enough that he asks, "Are you there?" I say, "Sure."

I doubt he's suddenly decided to tell me what was going on, but I might as well get a meal out of him.

We don't talk, except to the waitress, until we've got coffee and waffles in front of us.

Nick reaches for the sugar. "You know, I'm not good at the family thing."

I roll my eyes. "Understatement."

"No, really. The idea that anyone would even care where I was going, or what I was doing—it's just mind-boggling. I can't get used to it. So I'm sorry if I seemed angry earlier."

"It's okay," I say, making loopy designs on my waffles with the syrup.

I've let him get away with it again. Whatever "it" is.

"I'm going to try harder," Nick says. "I know I disappoint people. It's easier not to let anyone in, you know? But you're my sister, and you came out here even though you knew basically *nothing* about what my life was like."

I still don't. Though I'm developing some theories.

I spear a bite of waffle.

"I can't tell you how much that means to me. And you've gotten so amazing—you can really act, you're totally together—"

"I can change a tire," I say, mimicking his animated tone.

I don't know why he's saying this stuff, but I can't deny I like hearing it.

"Right, totally! So that's all, just, man. It's a little intimidating, I tell you. My little sister, you've become like the queen of competence."

"You're such a damn liar."

Nick shakes his head. "No, really. Trust me."

And I can't explain why, but while we're sitting there, eating our stupid waffles in the middle of the night, I do.

scene ii

THE SUN WAKES me, hot squares of light coming through the panes of my window, making it red behind my eyes. By the time we got home last night, everyone was asleep or elsewhere. It felt like sneaking in after curfew. Nick knocked over a plant and swore, and it made us laugh, shush each other, then laugh more. Before we went to bed, Nick hugged me, for the first time since the day I got here.

I stretch, then get up. No way I can keep sleeping, it's too bright. Maybe I need curtains.

Charles is downstairs, lying on the reclaimed sofa. Someone finally propped the missing leg with a cinderblock.

He takes his headphones off. "He's gone again."

I run a hand through my hair and look toward the back porch, where Meryl usually has her first cigarette of the day.

Charles follows my gaze. "So is she. Isn't it interesting how that happens?"

"They probably had to work. Is there coffee?"

"If you make some. Where did you and your brother go last night? Ms. Meryl was worrying. She smoked even more than usual."

My heart beats faster. "How do you know? You came back outside?"

"Eventually."

"I thought fireworks bothered you."

"Certain other things bother me more."

"What things?"

"Oh," Charles says, "you know. The usual. Make enough for two, would you?"

While the coffee brews, I take two mugs from the row of cup hooks. "You like cream and sugar, right?"

"And you don't," Charles says. "I'll get up and doctor my own coffee, you don't have to."

"Okay."

Charles comes into the kitchen. "I stir the cream and sugar together before I put the coffee in. It blends better. Like simple syrup. You know, before you got here, I didn't think I'd like you at all. I didn't even think you were really his sister."

"Why not?"

Charles looks at me. "Well, once I *saw* you, it was harder to think you weren't, but when he was just *talking* about it, I thought, right, Nick wants to get some chick in the house, whatever, that's happened before, he seems to need to, uh, prove himself every so often."

"But I thought you were . . ."

"I thought we were, too."

He smiles unhappily.

I pour myself a cup, then hand the coffeepot to Charles. After he adds coffee to his sweetened cream, he raises his cup to me in a toast. Then he picks up a watering can, fills it from the sink, says, "Thanks," raises the can in a second toast, and goes out the back door. I follow him.

Outside, it's hot enough that I immediately start to sweat. Charles waters the plants on the porch from the can. Then he turns on the hose to douse the rest of the yard.

"When it's like this out," he says, "I always water early. Otherwise the water just boils everything, and it all shrivels and dies. Learned that the hard way."

"I wouldn't have known that," I say. "My mother would be deeply *upset* that I didn't know that, but nonetheless."

"Hmmm. Mom likes gardening. That's appropriate for a nice Southern lady. What does your dad like?"

"Telling people what to do. Making them feel better."

"Shrink?"

Why doesn't he know this? Hasn't Nick told him? "Minister."

Charles whistles. "Explains a lot."

"Does it?"

Charles spins slowly, like the ballerina on a music box, directing the hose's spray to different parts of the garden. "He's the bad boy. You're the good girl."

"What makes me good?"

"Please," Charles says. "You've got, what, two months before you start at a superswank college? You could fuck up a lot in two months. But—you don't smoke, you barely drink, you seem uninterested in psychoactive drugs, you do the dishes, you don't make messes in the common areas, you have a progressive, socially responsible job, you pay your share for everything on time—should I go on? Are you volunteering at the cancer ward, too?"

"They do worry. And there's a lot they don't know."

"Really? I thought you'd overcompensate for Nick and tell them everything."

"Even if I wanted to tell them, there's a lot they don't want to hear."

Charles shuts off the hose.

"Turn off the sun while you're at it, would you, dear?" It's Aurora, pale and squinting, shielding her eyes, her white silk kimono wrapped around her like a shroud. She fishes in her pocket, brings out cigarettes and a lighter.

"Thought you said last night you were quitting," Charles says.

"Blood vessels," Aurora says. "Need to thin them out. Reduce pressure."

"Why don't you drink some water?" He fills the watering can from the hose and holds it out to her. She waves it away.

"Did. And took vitamins. I'll be fine. I've been getting hangovers since before you were born."

"That's what concerns me," Charles says. He kneels on the now-damp ground and begins to pull up weeds.

Aurora looks old this morning, yesterday's makeup faded and smeared, wrinkles prominent in the unforgiving sunlight.

She catches me looking. "I try to present as hideous a morning-after figure as possible, to discourage others from sin. I trust I've been successful once again."

"I wasn't—" I lie.

"It's fine. At the moment I am an apparition. But when you see me later, after I put myself back together, you will doubt the former evidence of your own eyes."

Charles sighs. "Oh, Margo. You're such a queen. It was a bumpy night, wasn't it?"

"At least the explosions have ceased," Aurora says.

Several children scream with delight as someone sets off another bottle rocket. Aurora winces.

"Battle," Charles says. "What are you doing right now?"

"Not much."

"Come with me to the costume shop and we'll get you measured. We both seem to have some unexpected free time, and we might as well use it."

THE COSTUME SHOP, in the theater basement, is only a little larger than a closet. The space resembles an overstuffed low-end resale shop, with lots of costumes hanging too close together on the beat-up racks, others in piles on the floor, still others in an ancient, open steamer trunk shoved into one corner. Dozens of blank styrofoam heads, each one wearing a hat or a wig, line the shelves mounted to the walls. Everything seems to be organized, as far as that goes, by historical era, and there's a slight scent in the air of mothballs, mustiness, and sweat. There's just enough room for Charles and me to stand.

"Once we're finished with this part, there's a few things I'll want you to try on," Charles says. "Now we'll get your waist and hips," he goes on. "Note that your actual waist is above the waistline of your jeans."

I hold my arms out so Charles can continue measuring.

"Hmm," he says, holding up the tape measure. "I bet you could fit into the costumes Nick's worn for other shows. Did you know that your hips are only an inch wider than your brother's?"

"No. Should I have?"

Charles laughs. "It's just very, very strange, how much the two of you look alike."

"Well, we *are* related."

"Yes. Do you guys look more like your mom or your dad?"

"Dad, I guess. He's tall."

"Reverend Dad," Charles says, with evident satisfaction. "What does he think of your involvement in the bohemian world of the theater?"

"He was an actor for a long time himself," I say. "It's not like he's from a different *planet*."

"Sorry. He must be from one of the enlightened denominations. And preaching is another kind of performing, certainly. Turn around."

"How long have you known Nick?" I ask, tired of answering questions.

"In the biblical sense?" Charles asks brightly. He kneels, so he can measure my thigh.

I'm glad he's not looking at my face. "Yes. Sure."

"Why, it was a scene not unlike this one—"

"Okay, stop."

"You asked."

"You're right, I did."

"I won't continue to shock your delicate sensibilities with the details, but I will say it was during a show. Surprise, surprise!"

"Was it a while ago?"

"Yes. But it burns in my memory with a gemlike flame."

"I'm sorry," I say.

"Don't be. It's nothing to do with you."

LATER THAT DAY, at rehearsal, a slippery spot on the stage causes Demetrius to fall on his ass, and it's hard not to laugh, so Aurora decides to work the fall into the blocking for the scene. Lysander still doesn't have his lines.

"Hey—can I get a ride home from you?" Meryl asks, when I'm getting ready to leave. "I didn't think I was gonna make it today. My truck died."

"Yeah, I guess I can drive you. It's not like it's out of my way," I say, careful not to sound especially pleased. "What happened to the truck?"

"Oh, it was ugly. I had the radio cranked like always, and then suddenly it was silent, but you know, it's community radio and sometimes someone's just high and forgets to have the next song cued up. So I didn't think about it until a couple minutes later when the engine started making these horrible clunking sounds—I just barely got off the road in time. And I can't afford to get it towed, so it's just sitting there on the street, waiting for any passing tweaker to smash the window and grab the stereo. Not that the stereo's worth anything, but that won't matter, because, hey, it can be pawned."

"That sucks. I could loan you enough to get it to a mechanic," I offer. We get into my car. Meryl shakes her head vigorously and says, "Thanks, but no. I stopped loaning or borrowing money."

"So what are you going to do?"

"Abandon it. There's no other real option."

"Where is it?"

"It's on Failing. Perfect, huh?"

"Ha. Failing. So do you need a ride to work tomorrow?"

Can I manufacture another excuse to spend time with you?

"That would be great. I was planning on walking, but. Yeah, thanks. I don't suppose you could get me to rehearsal later, too?"

"Of course," I say.

And I'll be expecting some quid pro quo.

Except not.

scene iii

WHEN SOMEONE TEACHES swimming, and it's summer, it makes complete sense for her to wear a bathing suit and really short shorts to work. It isn't appropriate to gawk. Even though Meryl's bathing suit has a halter top that ties at the back of her neck, and it's very hard not to imagine what would happen if the tie loosened.

But I'm supposed to be driving.

Meryl unwraps two pieces of gum and puts them both in her mouth. "Want some? I always chew a bunch of gum before work, so the little guys won't be able to smell my cigarette breath."

"You could quit. Then you wouldn't have to buy gum *or* cigarettes. Think of the money you'd save."

"Think of how much less happy I'd be," Meryl says. The scent of spearmint fills the car. "The gum's a little bit of over-kill, really—I think the chlorine kills every other smell."

"Did you start smoking because of Aurora?"

Meryl laughs. "Are you kidding? We started talking the first time because *she* wanted a cigarette and she bummed one from me. I don't even remember where we were—a party maybe?"

"Is she close to anybody that's her own age? Besides Robert, I mean?"

Meryl hits me lightly on the leg. "Judgmental much? Aurora has all kinds of friends. She's interested in connecting with people. It's creepy if someone only spends time with other people their exact same age. You should always have people older and younger than you in your life."

"I know, but—"

"Listen. It was Aurora who tipped the scales for you to be

able to move in. I knew a few different people who needed a space after Callie moved out, and I'm pretty sure Robert did, too. But Nick promised everyone that you'd be coming, and that you only needed the room for a few months, so she decided she'd leave it open until you got out here. So cut her a little slack."

"I didn't know that."

"I know you didn't. Hey, this is the parking lot. Thanks for the ride."

The pool where Meryl teaches is indoors, but the building has huge windows, so I can see the entire pool clearly from the parking lot.

The little guys love Meryl. She seems to know just how long they can be expected to concentrate on something hard like putting their faces in the water. After they work for a while, she lets them jump up and down and splash each other, and she gives them piggyback rides.

Then she looks out toward the parking lot, and I feel like a stalker, so I turn the key in the ignition and drive away.

I look up Failing in the Thomas Guide—it's not far away. So I drive over there and discover that despite its name, Failing is a quiet, pretty, tree-lined street. But when I find the truck, sure enough, Meryl's passenger-side window is shattered, and the stereo's gone. Broken glass glitters on the ground next to the car.

I call the road-service number on my insurance card. When the guy shows up, the first thing he says is, "Damn, that's a shame. They get anything besides the stereo?"

"No," I say, although I have no idea what else Meryl might've had in the truck.

"So, it won't start, right? You need a jump?"

"No—I tried that, it didn't work, that's why I called," I lie. If he was going to try jump-starting it, he'd need the keys, which, of course, I don't have. My voice sounds all shaky. I hope he'll just assume I'm upset because the truck's both non-functional and burglarized. I'm not as good at this as Nick is.

"All right then. Where d'you want it towed?"

"Where would you recommend? I'm new in town and I can't afford to spend a lot."

He names a place. For all I know, his brother owns it and they'll charge the earth.

"Sure," I say, and we go.

When we get to the mechanic's, they ask for the keys, and I "panic." "I don't know—I don't know where they are, oh my God, maybe I dropped them back there? Oh, no—and my house keys are on there, too!"

The mechanics are sympathetic.

"Don't worry," the guy who's going to fix Meryl's truck says. "We can make some new ones."

By the time I walk back to my own car—stereo intact in

the glove compartment—then drive to Forest House, all I want to do is take a shower, then a nap before I pick up Meryl for rehearsal.

But Nick's outside, and when he sees me pull up, he waves and says, "Hey! Want to learn some things that'll be really useful for your acting?"

"Sure," I say. This is the first time since our coffee and waffles the night of the Fourth that he's shown any signs of wanting to hang out with me.

"You ever done any stage combat?"

"I've only been in one other play. Besides, it doesn't seem like girls in Shakespeare fight that much." I wipe sweat from my forehead.

"You're forgetting Hermia and Helena's fight in Three, Two."

Act Three, Scene Two. Theater jargon.

"They don't *hit* each other, they just trade insults."

"*Totally* depends on the director. Aurora might want you two to really go at it. Which would be hot, frankly."

I frown, but Nick goes on.

"Yeah, I think the audience could really go for you guys, oh, wrestling some, maybe—there'd be a nice contrast, you know, tall and short, blonde and brunette. . . ."

I can see it in my head.

I've been seeing it in my head for days.

"She hasn't said anything about anything like that."

"Well, she's put on some pretty physical productions in the past. In fact, Meryl and I hooked up during one of them—she was a *fun* shrew to tame, let me tell you!"

Nick laughs.

"This stage combat," I say carefully, "how does it work? Do I hit you?"

"No. It just looks like you do. It's not the truth, it's not reality. But it's a *theatrical* truth."

"I don't think I'd be any good at that."

"Sure you would. You've done a lot of dancing, right? It's like that—it's all about control. Focusing your movements, leading the audience to see what you want them to see."

"Sounds like you have a lot of experience."

"I do. And trust me, it's a lot harder *not* to hurt someone than it is to hurt them."

I ponder this, and he continues. "We're going to need to go inside. I've got a mat that'll be a lot softer than this dry ground. First thing you're going to learn is how to roll."

"Um, I took gymnastics before ballet, in case you forgot. And doesn't everyone know how to do a forward roll?"

I turn a somersault, to demonstrate.

Nick shakes his head. "A stage-combat roll is totally different. Watch."

Nick rolls, leading with his shoulder. It's a more diagonal movement, not down the center of the spine.

"Looks easy," I say.

"It's supposed to. But you're gonna need to practice it a bunch of times before you do it outside, okay? I don't want you getting injured."

I roll the way Nick did.

"Or not," Nick says. "That was good!"

"It's also boring. Let's fight. If I hit you, you can block it, right?"

I throw an awkward punch, a left jab that doesn't come anywhere near Nick's face. He laughs.

"If you're gonna punch like that, I don't even *have* to block it."

I punch again, aiming for his stomach. He deflects my arm with his, throwing me off balance.

"Wait a minute, I think I'm detecting some genuine hostility here. What's going on?"

I try again, a kick this time. He moves fluidly out of the way.

"Why can I never *get* to you?" My voice comes out louder and higher than I want it to.

"Well, for starters, you're totally trying too hard. You'd think you really wanted to beat me up! What did I ever do to you?"

I grab his T-shirt. It rips.

"What the hell is your problem today?"

I say nothing. I'm trying not to cry.

Nick chuckles, low and deep in his throat.

"Oh, *now* I get it," he says.

"What do you *get?*"

Nick smiles. "So, you ready? Learning to roll is just the beginning. If you keep going with this, before you know it, you'll be able to punch and kick and strangle, all without leaving marks!"

"Great. Let's do it."

"First, don't think of a white horse," Nick says.

"What?"

"It's a martial-arts thing. Don't think of a white horse. Quick, what are you thinking of right now?"

You and Meryl together. "A white horse."

"Exactly! But you can't do that! So shake it off, okay? Whatever it is."

WE'RE TWENTY MINUTES into rehearsal before I remember that I was supposed to pick up Meryl. Oh, the irony.

"Sorry I'm late. My ride flaked and I had to walk," Meryl says, glaring at me. Her hair is damp, her T-shirt sweaty. I open my mouth, but before I can get a word out, Aurora says, "Well, I'm sorry about that, but you really need to make getting here on time a priority. You knew it was a lover night, and that we'd be finalizing the blocking for Three, Two."

"Yep, I knew it," Meryl says, twisting her hair into a loose knot. "It won't happen again."

I put my hand on her arm, but she knocks it away.

"Okay, let's go from Lysander and Helena's entrance. I want you all to keep what we've been doing in mind, but just move the way you feel your characters would move, and we'll see what choices we want to stay with."

Lysander finally has his lines. He acts like a cheerful, oblivious drunk—appropriate for someone who's just been given a love potion.

And it's no stretch for me to be as angry and frustrated as Helena needs to be; tired, bedraggled, convinced that everyone's making fun of her. Meryl-Hermia comes on, just as exhausted and worried, looking for her sweetheart, then finding out that he's not her sweetheart anymore, that—as she sees it—her friend Helena has betrayed her. Except that the way Helena sees it, it's the other way around, and Hermia's the one who's in the wrong, mocking her with the boys.

Aurora reminded us early on that the *audience* knows that the lovers are all mixed up because of Puck. So in a lot of productions, she said, the anger and the betrayal are broad and played for big laughs, as are the lovers generally. "But I want you to be thinking about other directions the energy could go," she'd said. There hadn't *been* any other directions, because Lysander still needed prompts and Demetrius was mumbly and the whole sequence wasn't *there*.

But now it feels real—two girls more angry and upset at each other than at the clueless boys around them, who really aren't the point. *Neither of us is acting,* I think in the moment before I say, "I evermore did love you, Hermia!" and then go on with the speech about going back to Athens because everything's so messed up.

Meryl pushes me so hard I have to take two steps backward. "Why, get you gone! Who is't that hinders you?"

"A foolish heart, that I leave here behind."

"What, with Lysander?"

I take Meryl by the shoulders and stare into her eyes. "With . . ."

I have to finish the line.

I drop my voice to say, "Demetrius."

Then I turn away.

It's the wrong way to play it. It's unlike anything Shakespeare, or Aurora, would want. Soon I'll have to shoehorn myself into the physical comedy of tall girl versus short girl.

But for right now, it's the closest I can get to an apology.

At the end of rehearsal, I go up to Meryl.

"Want a ride home?"

"Oh, no," Meryl says. "I figured I'd walk, since it was so much fun earlier. I mean, it wasn't like I had to *be* anywhere at a particular *time* or anything."

"I'm so sorry about before, I just—"

"Don't bother making up some story to explain. Just take me back to the house and don't talk to me."

Meryl opens my glove compartment and digs through it for the stereo faceplate. She shoves it on, scans until she finds something discordant with a lot of bass, and cranks the volume.

I don't mind that she doesn't want to talk. The music's all right, too.

But aside from the fact that she's pissed, I have no idea what's going on in Meryl's head.

Which was never the case with Nic.

I could read her like a book.

scene iv

I KEEP TRYING to find a chance to tell Meryl that I'm getting her truck fixed. But every time I see her, she finds some reason to be going the other direction. It's exactly like when I'm canvassing, and people have no qualms about crossing the street to avoid me.

So the day the truck is ready, I just drive it—using the new set of keys the mechanic made—over to Forest House, figuring I'll come up with some way to corner her and explain.

It's my night to make dinner. As usual, the prospect of food unites the house like nothing else. Everyone except Meryl, who's no doubt walking home from work, has converged in the kitchen to watch me cook.

"Isn't that Meryl's truck outside? I thought it was dead," Charles says, stealing a handful of chopped red peppers and tossing them into his mouth.

"It's fixed now," I say.

"Where'd she get the cash? She told me she was strapped." Nick grabs a slice of portobello.

"Would you guys quit it? There won't be enough to stir-fry if you keep eating it all raw."

When did she tell him?

"What the hell is my truck doing in the driveway?" Meryl demands.

"Move it if you want. It's fixed." I scrape the vegetables from the cutting board into the wok. They sizzle.

"Excuse me?"

"It's fixed. It was no big deal," I say, glancing up from the wok.

"How much do I owe you?" Her voice is clipped, like she's talking through clenched teeth. Maybe she is.

"It's no big deal," I say again.

"You know," my brother says, "my cab could really use

a tune-up. And some new shocks? Hook me up?"

"I've had my eye on a vintage Armani suit over at Avalon," Charles says. They laugh.

"Don't embarrass her, boys—it was a sweet, kind thing to do," Aurora says.

From the look in her eyes, if Meryl had a gun right now, I'd be bleeding.

"Just tell me how much it is," she says. "I'll write you a check."

"Hey, smells like dinner's burning," Robert says. "Better stir it."

"Thanks," I say, pushing food around with the wooden spoon. He nods and smiles—the first time he's ever smiled at me.

Too bad it wasn't him I was trying to impress.

I finish up the stir-fry and everyone serves themselves. When we're all seated around the kitchen table, Robert says, "Aurora and I, uh, we have an announcement."

Oh, now I know why he was smiling.

"Do I have a dress to design?" Charles asks.

Aurora says, "That won't be necessary, although I might ask for your help with some alterations."

She and Robert clasp each other's hands.

"You're going to do it soon?" Meryl asks. "Even with the show coming up and everything?"

"Well," says Aurora, "it's going to be a little challenging, but there are some circumstances that are, shall we say, adjusting the timeline rather dramatically—which is why we wanted to tell you all as soon as possible."

Charles chuckles. "What, is it *la migra?*" He takes a bite of the stir-fry.

Robert clears his throat. "Actually, yes. Not all of you know that I'm from Vancouver, and I'm here on a work visa. Which, we just found out, isn't going to be renewed."

"So they're finally cracking down on the goddamn Canucks taking vital set-design work from the American workingman?" Nick asks.

Robert shakes his head. "Nah, it's about the day job. But still."

"You'll be going to City Hall, then, right?" Meryl asks.

"Oh, no," says Aurora. "Absolutely not. We want a real ceremony, and we're going to make it happen."

"Why do I get the feeling that when you say 'we,' you mean the entire household?" Charles asks.

Aurora smiles. "Because you are *extremely* clever. But don't worry, it won't only be you all. We fully intend to rope in our entire acquaintance."

"What day is it going to happen?" I ask.

"Well, we have a friend who has a barn outside of town, and he'll let us use the space; some other friends have a band,

and they're willing to play for free drinks—we still need to find someone to perform the ceremony."

"Battle asked for the date," Charles points out.

Aurora puts her head in her hands. "You're all going to hate me, but we have no choice." She peeks out from between them and winces. "It'll be the day after our first full run-through with tech."

Everyone groans.

"When are you going to have the rehearsal?" I ask. I'm overly familiar with wedding logistics; an occupational hazard of being a preacher's kid.

Aurora says, "We're not going to have one. There's just no time. It'll just have to come together organically. But listen, one other thing—because it's so crazy, because we know we won't have time to do a lot of things that are traditional, and, well, just because we are who we are, we're not going to be requiring guests to wear any kind of *formal* dress, exactly—"

"The other shoe," says Charles. "I see it. It's poised in the air. I think—yes, I think it's about to drop . . ."

"No one will need to rent any tuxes, or buy any ridiculous dresses," says Robert.

"Oh, you two crazy kids—it's going to be a naked wedding!" Nick exclaims.

"No," Aurora says. "But everyone *will* have to wear a costume."

*   *   *

AT THE END of our next rehearsal, Aurora tells the rest of the cast about her suddenly fast-tracked wedding plans, and the surprising dress code.

"I used to think I'd marry you one day," Henry says, "and now, as a minister in the Universal Life Church, I'm pleased to say that I can." Aurora blushes and says she'd be honored to have him perform the ceremony. Oberon, whose real name is Damian, has a friend who works at that Lebanese restaurant we all like so much who'll probably cut them a deal on a buffet in return for ad space in the program. Titania, whose real name is Annalisa, works at a florist's shop and is confident that she can pull an arrangement together that won't cost much. Even the middle-school fairies volunteer themselves to sing Titania's lullaby during the ceremony. Everyone else starts scheming about what costume they're going to wear.

Aurora's thrilled, and even a little overwhelmed. She blinks away tears before clearing her throat and saying, "You are the best. I am so privileged to be able to work with all of you. Oh! I'm all choked up. But listen, I do have some more important information to give you. Remember that this coming weekend is our trip to the campground—Robert's printed up directions, and he's got a plan for splitting up who's bringing what for food and drink, so make sure to check in with him before you leave tonight."

Peaseblossom leans over to Titania/Annalisa and whispers a question. The answer is loud enough for everyone to hear:

"No, the campground is not going to have wi-fi! For God's sake, child, you can live without the Internet for one weekend!"

I hadn't realized that Titania was Peaseblossom's mom. Now that I know, I see the resemblance. They're both blonde, and they have the same small, pointed nose. Their voices are similar, too. When the two of them are waiting for the rest of the fairies to be ready to leave—since Titania's also the designated fairy chauffeur—they stand the same way: left foot slightly forward, weight on the back leg.

"Your cell phone won't work either, I'm afraid," Aurora says. "Can you stand it?"

"Well, actually," Peaseblossom says, "I'm waiting for callbacks for another show, so I'm a little concerned. I mean, do we really all need to be there?"

"I can't require it," Aurora says, "but I think everyone who goes will have a very good time." She's looking at Titania, not Peaseblossom.

"I haven't been camping in a long time," I confess, "and I don't have a tent."

"Mine's big enough for two," Meryl says. While I'm processing this information, she adds with extra emphasis, "It's *no big deal.*"

"Um, okay," I say, and she goes on, "You'd better ride up with me, too—after all, I wouldn't *have* a ride if not for you." She smiles and punches my arm.

ACT IV

Yeah, He's a Runner

scene i

BESIDES ALL OF Forest House, the people who end up being able to go on the trip are Oberon/Damian, Titania/Annalisa—she decided to leave Peaseblossom at her dad's house—and Bottom/Henry. Everyone else either has to work (Starveling, Peter Quince, Egeus, Flute, Demetrius), can't get permission from her parents (all the middle-school fairies except Peaseblossom—Mustardseed cried when she told Aurora that she couldn't come), or is "allergic to nature" (Snug, Lysander).

The campground's in the middle of a pine forest. It smells sharp and green. All the campsites are set back from a main road that leads to a beach. The sites are spaced far enough apart that each one feels private.

The only drawback is that it's crowded with families, some of whom think the outdoors is a perfect place to test the capacity of their recreational vehicles' sound systems.

"I thought the point of going camping was to get *away* from shit like that," Charles says. He puts his headphones on, and Nick laughs and takes them off, saying, "You're such a hypocrite! Just because they're not blasting *your* favorites. Come on, expand your horizons!"

"They're expanding. I'm sleeping on the ground, aren't I?"

"Stop bitching. You're going to be in a fabulous high-tech tent. You'll barely know you're outside."

"Oh, I'll know." Charles puts on his headphones again, and sings, "'It will be too late by the time we learn / what these cryptic symbols mean.'"

Henry has just finished setting up his large red tent.

"*This* is *exactly* what I *needed!*" He throws out his arms as if he intends to hug the entire campsite.

Then he unfolds a blue canvas camp chair, takes a can of beer out of his cooler, and sits in the chair, propping his legs up on the cooler as though it's an ottoman. He pops open the beer and takes a long gulp.

"Ahh—I won't be moving for the next few hours. You young ones can sear me some marshmallows later."

Meryl pokes him in the leg. "No marshmallows for you, not if you're gonna block access to the beer."

"Shocked, I'm shocked that you would even *think* of desiring such access. An infant such as yourself."

"Yeah," Meryl says, sitting in Henry's lap, "the same infant you were making daiquiris for at the last cast party. Give it up, old man." She kisses him on the top of his head.

"Good lord. That was you? She seemed like such a pleasant, unassuming creature."

Meryl ruffles Henry's hair, gets off his lap, and raises his legs so she can get a beer from the cooler. I think about asking Meryl to get one for me, too, but it's early yet. Better to be clear-headed, at least to start with.

"Marshmallows. Annalisa, you're signed up for them. You got 'em?" Robert asks. He has a clipboard and a printout that lists each food item people said they'd bring, with boxes to check off when he's verified that the item has made it to the site.

"Not only do I have marshmallows, I have graham crackers *and* Ghirardelli chocolate, since my darling daughter isn't around to tell me I shouldn't be eating it."

"Ghirardelli in s'mores is a waste," Damian says. "It's like using filet mignon in your meat loaf."

Damian also has a large tent. His is dark green. He's brought several kinds of cheese, two loaves of bread that he baked himself, a few bottles of wine, and a dozen wineglasses—*glass* glasses, packed in bubble wrap. "I absolutely will not stand for anyone drinking wine from a plastic cup," he says when he unwraps them. "It's a travesty."

Meanwhile, Aurora is scribbling furiously in her note-books. She has two, a red one and a blue one. The red one is for the show. The blue one, I'm assuming, is for the wedding. She hasn't stopped muttering to herself since we got here.

During the drive from Portland, Meryl talked a lot. I didn't. She kept telling stories about people she knew from past shows that ended with "You know how that goes, right?" or "You know what I'm talking about" or "You know how it is."

I kept nodding and saying, "Yeah." But more than half the time, I didn't.

"Nick!" Robert calls. My brother is nearly out of earshot, walking toward the beach. He turns and smiles.

"You're doing the entrée tonight—salmon, you said?" Robert asks. "And steak for those of us who aren't fish fans? And eggplant for the vegetarians?"

Nick slaps his hand to his forehead. "Damn! Yes, Robert, you're right, I did sign up for the entree. And I got some beautiful fish, and a fantastic cut of beef, and eggplant that was positively voluptuous. But I'm afraid that it's all sitting on the counter, back at Forest House."

"Oh, God," Meryl says. "The kitchen will be totally infested by the time we get back."

I don't think so.

That would imply that the food existed in the first place.

"You're so right. I'm so sorry. Tell you what, I'll catch a ride back early and clean it all up so the rest of you won't have to deal with it. God, I can't believe I did that. Ugh, how awful."

Robert says, "So. What are we going to eat tonight, then?"

Nick says, "I'll figure out something. It's totally my responsibility—"

"Yes, it is," Robert says.

"I know, I know, so I'll totally figure out something. I promise you, no one will be going hungry tonight." Nick aims his last sentence at Robert's prominent stomach. I can't tell if Robert notices, since he's already glaring.

Aurora looks up from her notebooks to say, "Oh, we'll be fine. After all, there's Damian's bread and cheese, and the chocolate—and so much lovely liquor!" Then she hugs Robert, who makes a face, but hugs her back.

"Well, I'm going to go forage," Nick says. "Like the fellow said, I shall return."

"I'll go with you," I say quickly. "I can help carry, or whatever."

"Great!" Nick says. "Let's hit it." He stands up and heads for the road.

"Yeah, great," Meryl mutters. She sits on a stump and lights a cigarette. I hesitate for a minute, then follow Nick.

"So, foraging," I say when I catch up to him. "What's your strategy?"

"Wait and see."

A woman is gathering driftwood at the water's edge. Nick watches her for a while, then starts to gather wood himself. Not knowing what else to do, I do, too. The beach is littered with wood—thin branches and large stumps, all sun-bleached and pounded smooth by water and sand. I can't resist running my hands up and down one branch. It's so soft, it feels like skin.

When the woman stops and stoops to pick up what she's gathered, Nick slaps his forehead and says, "Oh, shit!" Then he approaches the woman and asks, "Excuse me, but could you use some more wood?"

"Sure," she says, "but don't you need it?"

Nick smiles and shrugs. "Well, you see, we *would* need it— if I'd remembered the food we were going to cook over the fire we were going to build—but I just this minute realized, I *forgot* it, and it's four hours away!"

He's increased the distance we traveled by an hour.

The woman says, "Oh, no, that's terrible! Do you have anything else you can eat?"

I open my mouth, shut it again. Nick says, "Nah, you know, we were so amped about getting out of town, you know, I can't believe it but we seriously just spaced packing up the food. So here"—he bends and picks up his pile of wood—"you should totally take this!"

The woman smiles. "You sure?"

"Absolutely."

"Okay, well, thanks so much! God, I hate to even ask this, I feel so bad for you, but I can't carry it all, so do you mind helping me get it back to our site?"

"Not at all."

The woman hasn't noticed me. I decide to stay put.

I sit down in the sand, leaning back on a rough stump. At this moment, no one knows where I am.

There's something magical about being by myself in a strange place. If I squint just right, even the dead jellyfish washed up on the beach turn into shimmering spots in the sand.

By the time Nick reappears, the sun is setting and it's cooler. He's got a heavy grocery bag.

"Hey, I lost you for a while there—good thing you didn't go anywhere. But now we're really close," he says. "Awfully nice girls. And the folks in the next site over weren't bad, either."

I get up, brushing sand from my jeans. "What did you *say* to them?"

Nick smiles. "Oh, you know."

"No, I don't."

"Let's get back. Robert will be gnawing off his own fleshy arm." Nick turns back toward the road.

"Why are you so mean to him?" I ask.

"It's not mean if it's true. Besides, surely you've noticed that he's less than thrilled with *my* presence on the planet."

"I think he's just not very comfortable around a lot of theater people."

"So he builds sets, why? Is marrying a director, why? Oh, hold on."

Nick slows down as we get close to another campsite. A bright red pickup with oversized tires is parked diagonally in front. The truck extends far enough into the road that it forces cars to drive into the grass to get around it. The truck bed is full of groceries. Just past the front end of the truck, there's a picnic table covered with cases of beer. No one's nearby.

"Hold this," Nick says, handing me the bag he's been carrying. Then he reaches into the truck bed and takes out the closest sack.

"Jesus! Put that back!"

"Nope," Nick says. He's already walking back toward our own campsite. "It's their own fault for leaving it all unattended. Besides, they're annoying!"

"You don't *know* they're annoying," I say, falling helplessly into step behind him.

"Please. Take a look back at that vehicle and tell me you'd want to spend quality time with the owners," Nick says, laughing.

"You don't even know what's *in* there."

"That's half the fun," Nick says. "It's a gamble! Don't peek now."

"I haven't peeked at all the *other* stuff you scammed."

"Ah, don't call it that," Nick says. "It was a performance. And that bag you're carrying? It's full of edible applause."

"Well, that's great. I hope it's filling, so you'll be fortified when the pickup people show up later to kick your ass."

"They won't even miss it. Come on! You saw how much beer they had. Once they get a few of those down their throats, they'll barely remember they brought food at all."

AURORA SEES US. "I *told* you they'd be back!"

No slurring yet. Her voice is a little loud, though.

"Well, I hope it suffices," Nick says.

The "edible applause" from the nice wood-gathering woman and her friends is summer sausage, scallops, and energy bars.

"Something for everyone!" says Aurora.

Robert shakes his head. "How are we going to prepare scallops?"

"We'll"—Nick rummages in the second bag—"wrap them in this tinfoil and cook them in the coals!"

He tosses the foil to Robert.

"Let's see, what do we have here . . . Damian, think fast!" Nick throws a bag of pretzels at him, football-style, and Damian catches it one-handed.

"Annalisa!" Fun-size Hershey bars.

"Meryl!" A cheese ball.

"Battle!" Olive loaf.

"Henry!" Hot-dog buns.

"But where, my friend, are the hot dogs?" Henry asks.

Back in the truck bed with the rest of those people's food, maybe?

Then Nick pulls out a package of tofu dogs, and tosses them at Charles, saying, "Eat your heart out, buddy!"

Everyone's laughing except Robert and me. Annalisa rips open the bag of Hershey bars and throws one at Damian. He hurls a handful of pretzels at her. Meryl says, "God, you people! Don't waste food! If you're going to throw something at someone, the other person has to catch it in their mouth!"

"Don't you be throwing that cheese ball at me, then, missy!" Damian says.

"Wait, there's more! Oh, well, *this* I won't presume to throw. I'll leave it right here, near my tent. Anyone who's curious can investigate later." Nick sets the bag down and continues, "So—I know that *I* wasn't signed up to bring firewood—which of y'all is it?"

Robert raises his hand. He's rolled a slice of olive loaf into the shape of a cigar. It's sticking out of the corner of his mouth.

"Then, dude," Nick asks, "why is there not a fire?"

Robert bites off a large portion of his rolled-up olive loaf and speaks with his mouth full. "Well, *dude*, I've spent the last few *weeks* building things for you people, and I was just taking a few minutes to appreciate the phenomenon of *not* building anything." He eats the rest of the olive loaf, gulps some beer, and belches.

"Say no more," Nick says. "I'll be your Prometheus."

"Does that mean we can tie you to a rock later and tear out your liver?" Meryl asks. Robert snickers.

"No," Nick says. "You can loan me your lighter, though."

Meryl throws it at him—hard. He catches it easily, one-handed like Damian.

Just once I wish he'd fumble.

I walk over to Henry, who's still using his cooler as an ottoman. Two empty cans stand next to it, and Henry looks correspondingly more mellow.

"May I have a beer?"

Henry moves his legs, opens the lid. I plunge my hand into the melting ice and retrieve a can. The cold stings my hand, but it's nice.

"Thanks!" I pop the can open, take a sip.

"You didn't give *her* any shit about having a beer! What's up with that?" Meryl pokes Henry in the ribs.

"Well, Miss Meryl, you'll note that *she* asked *nicely*."

"Hmf, *nice*. Nice doesn't get you very far."

"Apparently sometimes it gets you a beer," Damian says.

I watch Nick work on the fire. First he rips up one of the grocery sacks to use as kindling.

Why isn't anyone else wondering where the food came from?

I look at Meryl, who's deep in conversation with Annalisa.

Meanwhile Nick stacks branches to make a pyramid, then holds the lighter up to a piece of the ripped-up sack until a corner of it sparks. He blows on the spark, slow and controlled, and the spark spreads. "Come on," he coaxes. He blows again. One of the branches catches.

Even the damn fire does what he wants.

"I have to investigate your *mysterious item*!" Aurora announces. She picks up the bag, peeks in. "Well! Excellent, excellent—I don't see why you felt the need to be so *secretive*—everyone, in this bag, right here, there is a box of condoms. So should there be any eventuality where such an item might be required, now you know where to find them. And we promise not to gossip about who reaches into the bag, right?"

"Speak for yourself," Damian says.

Charles takes out his deck of cards, sits down at the picnic table, starts shuffling.

"You gonna share?" Nick asks.

Charles hands Nick the package of tofu dogs.

"No, no, I meant the cards. We've got hours before it gets dark. I bet we could get a fine game going. Hearts, anyone?"

"'Where are these hearts?'" Henry quotes.

"God, what is it with you and hearts? Why don't you just play poker on the Internet like everyone else in America?" Meryl asks.

"A wise man once said that poker is a man's game, because it isn't fair," Nick says. "I won't play that kind of game online. Or with friends."

"Sure, I'm in," Annalisa says.

"Let me play a hand of solitaire," Charles says. "Then it's all yours."

Damian sits opposite Charles. "Are you a professional? That's some fancy shuffling."

Charles laughs. "Try 'not having anything better to do for a long-ass time.' But thanks."

"I had to learn some tricks, way back when I was playing Nathan Detroit," Damian says. "The director thought it would add some visual interest, but whenever I had those cards in my hands, I thought I was gonna blow my lines, I had to concentrate so hard. Never got so it felt right."

"Race-blind casting for *Guys and Dolls*? Sounds interesting," Henry says.

"It was. Not a bad little show."

"Hey, everybody—what's your favorite part that you've ever played?" Meryl asks.

"You mean aside from what we're doing in this *Dream*? I'm

sure that would be *everyone's* choice," Henry says, grinning at Aurora, who raises her glass—one of Damian's—to him.

"You are such a suck-up, old man," Meryl says. "Okay, then, let's not do that. How about the *worst* show, the one you leave off your résumé and you hope no one ever finds out about? I'm sure we all have one, right?"

"This is only my second show," I say.

"Oh, my God!" Annalisa cries. "You're a baby!"

The fire's burning brightly now, but Nick still squats next to it. Every so often he adds another branch or uses a long stick as a lever to readjust the placement of one of the larger logs.

Damian stands up and clasps his hands behind his back.

"My Worst Show Ever, by Damian J. Wolf. I was known at the time of this sordid event as DJ Wolf. The show was one of those productions that had no purpose other than to make white people feel better about themselves. This lady— you know the type, you got the big clunky turquoise jewelry, the hippie skirts, the leotards, and the Palestinian scarf to demonstrate how she is down with all oppressed peoples everywhere—comes to my high school. And her job is to show all of us poor needy children how to Express Our Authentic Voices, and Tell the True Stories of the Street."

"Oh, no," Aurora says. "I bet she got a grant."

"Maybe so. Anyway, she tells us that what we're going to do is take a big, meaningful story, a classic! and rewrite it, to make it Relevant to Our Own Experience as Urban Youth. Don't you love how people say 'urban' when they mean black?"

"Tell me it wasn't *Romeo and Juliet*," Annalisa says.

"I can't tell you that, because I'd be lying. 'Yo, Romeo, why you gotta be like that?'"

"You were Romeo?" Meryl asks.

Damian shakes his head. "Friar Lawrence—or rather, Big L. He was a dealer."

"Of course," Henry says.

"I am so sorry," Meryl says. "God."

"Mine's worse!" Annalisa raises her hand.

Robert looks up. "I'd think that the *last* thing you'd all want to do with your time away is talk *more* about theater."

"Oh, come on—these are war stories!" Aurora says, putting her hand over Robert's mouth. "These are badges of honor! Annalisa, tell us yours."

Annalisa stands up. "*Steel Magnolias*. The director thought it would be innovative and meaningful to cast a *real* diabetic in the role of Shelby. Little did he know that not only was she a real diabetic, she was a real idiot, and had the lovely habit of forgetting to monitor her sugar levels. So. Opening night, in the middle of the second act, she goes into a real diabetic episode! And I blush to admit it, but it took me a while to figure it out, because she was so prone to overacting!"

"I'll tell you *my* worst," Robert says. "When the director changed her mind about the look of the production a week before opening, and we had to tear down the entire set and start over. And when I say 'we' I mean 'mostly me.'"

He frowns at Aurora, but you can tell he's not really mad. At least not anymore.

"I'm sorry, I'm sorry! I'll never do it again, I promise! But you have to admit that post-9/11, you have to think differently about *Richard the Third*," Aurora says.

"I admit nothing. And no, you won't. Because then you would have no set."

"And my bed would be cold and empty."

"That, too." They smile at each other.

I assess the distance between their tent and the one Meryl and I will be sharing. Probably not far enough away. I wish there were such a thing as a soundproof tent.

Charles says to Nick, "All right, I've finished. Did you still want to play?"

"Yes! Now who all's in? We need four, optimally. Annalisa, Charles—Henry?"

"Oh, good lord," Henry says. He lumbers over to the picnic table, holding his third beer. "It's been decades. Will you go over the rules?"

"Of course. And four is best, but five can work, too. Anyone else?" Nick asks.

"Sure," Robert says, surprising me.

Meryl says, "I have played all the hearts I need for this and my next several lifetimes."

"I can cook the sausage and tofu dogs if y'all want," I offer. Might as well destroy the evidence of my brother's latest theft.

"Not together!" Charles says.

"I'll help," Meryl says.

Aurora has a double camp chair—more like a camp sofa—and she stretches out on it, putting her hands behind her head. "This is so peaceful. You know, I shouldn't say this, because I really had wanted to run scenes, but I'm rather glad that so few of you were able to come."

"I won't tell Ellery you said that," Annalisa says.

"Darling Ellery. I hope she gets into that other show. What is it, again?"

"It's a new work. Local playwright. There's only one role for a girl her age, so she's been a little obsessed about it." Annalisa sighs.

"And you're so good, not being a stage mom! I'm proud of you."

Annalisa shudders. "I *had* a stage mom. I'm breaking the cycle of abuse."

The fire could use some more wood. I reach down to the pile stacked next to it and place a large log on top.

The structure Nick built collapses. A shower of sparks and smoke rises. I stare at it, not knowing what to do.

"Oh, that's gonna go out in a second," Meryl says. She starts kicking the logs and branches back into a pyramid shape.

"Don't burn yourself!" Annalisa says.

"No worries. These boots are industrial strength."

"Okay," Nick says. He rubs his hands together and smiles. "Ladies and gentlemen, the rules for hearts. It's a trick-taking game. You want as few points as possible. Hearts add to your score—which you don't want—and so does the Queen of Spades. She adds thirteen points."

"'Beware of the Queen of Spades! Her black widow's curse might find you yet,'" Robert sings, surprisingly melodic.

"Robert! Wouldn't have figured you for a Styx fan. I thought you only liked that yeedle-deedle shit," says Damian.

"Wouldn't have figured you for one, either," Robert says.

"Yeah, well, you know," says Damian. "I live to defy y'all's expectations."

Nick picks up the deck and shuffles. "We start by dealing all the cards evenly," he says, doing so. "Then everyone passes three cards to the player to their left. First card played is the two of clubs, and then we continue clockwise until everyone's played a card, and the highest card wins. Follow suit if you can, but if you don't have any clubs, you can play any card from your hand. But you can't lead a heart until after a heart's been played—and that's called 'breaking hearts.'"

"This is sounding a little too much like my love life," Annalisa says.

"One more rule," Nick says. "If you take all the hearts, plus the Queen of Spades, you shoot the moon. Then you can subtract twenty-six points from your own score, or add twenty-six points to everyone else's."

"Shoot the moon," Aurora says dreamily. "Would it bleed, do you think? I think it would. I think it would bleed . . . shooting stars."

"I think you'd better slow down," Robert says. He gets up from the picnic table, walks over to the camp sofa, and takes the glass from her hand.

I move closer to Meryl. "How'd you learn to build fires?"

"Girl Scout training, baby. Weren't you ever a Girl Scout?"

"I always had ballet."

"No shit, really? No offense, but I always heard that dancers were kind of nervous and fucked up."

"And anorexic. I know. It's not inevitable, but yeah. I've known a bunch of girls who were like that."

"So why haven't I seen you dance?" Meryl asks. She smiles.

I flash back to the night, more than a year ago now, that Nic played her viola and I danced. If I shut my eyes, I can almost hear the dark, sweet music.

But it's very far away.

"I stopped."

"Why?"

"It wasn't me. I thought it was for a long time, but it wasn't."

"Let's make this interesting!" Nick's voice is louder than usual. "Annalisa, you are keeper of the marshmallows, am I correct?" He smiles.

"Yes I am. Ooh, that's what we should be doing! I even brought skewers!"

"Excellent," Nick says. "Would you dole out five marshmallows to each of us? Then every time someone wins a hand, we all have to turn over a marshmallow. What do you say?"

"The sweet, gummy taste of success," Henry says. "Certainly. And the losers will maintain cholesterol levels lower than their batting averages. An excellent trade-off."

"Oh, Henry, good God, don't talk about cholesterol. We're here to *enjoy* ourselves!" Annalisa says. She breaks off a piece from the Ghirardelli chocolate bar and pops it into her mouth.

"None of the rest of you are old enough for such things to matter, I realize. But I, as Miss Meryl never fails to mention, am an old man, and I am compelled to concern myself with matters of health."

"Which is why you've been guzzling the beer nonstop," Meryl says.

"Beer is different. Beer doesn't stick in your teeth and cause decay."

Annalisa distributes the marshmallows. Charles arranges his like a castle, four in a circle, the fifth on top like a turret.

Eventually, Nick wins all the marshmallows, and stuffs them into his mouth one by one, not waiting to chew and swallow. The white goo hanging from the corners of his lips makes him look like a mad dog.

AFTER EVERYONE'S EATEN, and the fire's dying down, and the stars are beginning to be visible through the trees, it gets quiet. Robert's giving Aurora a backrub. Henry's wearing a miner's headlamp, reading a fat book called *The Deptford Trilogy*. Annalisa's asleep on the camp sofa, snoring softly. Charles is teaching Damian some new ways to shuffle. Nick's wandered off—allegedly just to the latrine, but he's been gone for a while.

Meryl and I are still next to the fire. Meryl's smoking. We've been silent for some time.

"Why do you smoke?" I ask.

"Well, it's mostly for the health benefits."

"Ha ha. But it's so gross. I don't get it."

"Don't you ever want to leave?"

"Leave where?"

"Like a boring party. Or any situation, really. You can hold up your pack and say, 'I'll be right back.' Total escape."

"Bullshit. If you want to leave, you can go to the damn bathroom."

Way to go, Battle: puritanical outrage is *so* sexy.

Meryl sighs, stands up, kicks a still-burning branch. "Oh, yeah, I know I have to stop. We *all* know we have to stop. Funny how knowing something's a bad idea doesn't make a difference."

She tosses her cigarette into the fire. Then she crumples the pack and throws that in, too. The cellophane smells acrid when it catches. There's a lot of smoke.

"You're out already?"

Meryl shakes her head.

"It *is* bullshit. I know it is. A crutch. A habit. A poison. La la la. In five minutes, I'll probably be *so* pissed that I threw them away. And I'll blame you."

"Okay. I don't mind."

Meryl stands up. "Let's go for a walk. It's pretty out. It'll distract me from my lack of chemicals."

"Sure. Down to the beach?"

Meryl nods.

We walk awhile without talking.

"So why is it," Meryl asks, kicking a stone in front of her, "that you can be all self-righteous at *me*—and you're totally justified, I'm not arguing that—and yet I have never once heard you call your brother on any of his shit?"

"Which shit would that be?" I ask. There are so many options.

It's gotten darker, and chilly. I can hear thumping bass from a nearby campsite, like a giant's heartbeat.

"*Any* of it," Meryl says. "You know what he does."

Some of it.

"Why doesn't anyone else? Why don't you?"

"You're the only one he'll listen to."

"I don't know about that."

"Trust me. You're his sister! You have a better chance of getting through to him than anyone else."

If by "better" you mean "worse."

I don't say anything, though. It's almost sweet, knowing that she thinks my good opinion matters to Nick.

Some women have built a bonfire on the beach. One has a guitar. I expect them to be drunk, but as we get closer, I don't see any bottles. Just women singing. Their voices rise clear and sweet into the night air.

We stop and sit in the sand a little ways away to listen.

Meryl says, "You never hear people do that anymore. It's like everyone's too intimidated by the radio or TV or something. It used to be this huge part of our culture. I've read about it—like, in the nineteenth century, lots of people had pianos, and they'd buy the *sheet music* for the hot new song, and people would gather around the piano and sing it together."

I nod, still listening.

The song ends. There's laughter. Someone says, "Woo!" Some jangled chords from the guitar, and then two of the women start kissing. None of the others pay the couple much attention.

I glance over at Meryl. Her face is slightly flushed.

"They didn't do so much of *that* in the nineteenth century," I say. They're still kissing. The one with longer hair is now sitting in her girlfriend's lap.

"Yeah they did," Meryl says, "they just called it romantic friendship, and it was okay as long as they still got married and had kids and everything. I read about that, too."

Meryl pulls the elastic from her ponytail and runs her hands through her hair, messing it up. Her face is very near mine. Somehow everything's become charged.

"Romantic friendship?" I ask.

Meryl puts her hands on the back of my neck, pulls me close, and kisses me. Her tongue thrusts into my mouth. Is she kissing me because she wants to smoke?

It's so unlike the way it was with Nic. I'm so not in control. My lips feel bruised. Meryl moves her hands to the small of my back, then under my T-shirt. I draw in my breath, and then her hands are on my breasts, and I gasp.

"What?"

"Your hands are freezing." I'm amazed I can speak.

"Then warm them."

I don't know why this is happening, I don't even know why I'm *letting* it happen, except that it's lovely, like I don't need to know what's coming next, like my job is to gasp and writhe and moan, and so that's what I do, I let myself go.

The woman with the guitar starts to play another song. She sings by herself this time, her voice a low alto. I can barely hear her over the constant pounding of the waves and the roar of the wind, which has picked up speed and gotten even colder.

Soon I forget about the cold.

"I DIDN'T MEAN for that to happen," Meryl says, later.

Wait, that's what I was going to say.

Or not say. Just think.

"Look," Meryl continues, "you know what happened before, right?"

I stay silent.

"You do. With me and Nick. You know about that."

"Some. Not a lot."

"So, how fucked up and pervy does that make this?"

I shrug. I wish she'd shut up.

Meryl sits up and yanks her hair back into its ponytail.

"I mean, God," she goes on, "I'll cop to being kind of a ho.

It's just the way I am. A girl has needs. But after everything that went down with Nick, it's a miracle that I'm still in the same house with him. And who the hell do I decide to hook up with next? His fucking *sister*. Another in my continuing series of brilliant life choices."

I pull Meryl's ponytail. "Right, because I'm *so much* like him."

Part of me wonders what she means by "everything," but conversation is not my top priority at the moment.

"I know, I know you're not, although you do look a lot alike—I'm sorry but you do—and *that's* weird; it makes it all feel even more against the rules and messed up and I mean, I don't know, I don't know if I can really handle the idea of—"

I push Meryl down onto the sand again.

ONCE IT REALLY does get too cold to stay on the beach, we walk back to the campsite without saying anything.

Henry's the only one awake. He's still reading, still wearing his miner's headlamp. Since he's wearing all black, he looks like a floating head. He raises his eyes from the book when he sees us. "Hello, infants."

"Hi, old man," Meryl says.

"Hmm," Henry says. "I was going to say you missed the excitement, but perhaps you didn't."

"What excitement?" Meryl asks.

"The nice park ranger, or whatever his official title may be, came by and warned us that there might be bears around. Apparently some food's gone missing from a few of the sites, from people silly enough to leave it out, uncovered. So did you have any run-ins with large mammals? Nick was concerned. He went to look for the two of you. But I was confident, Miss Meryl, that you could defend yourself."

"I'm flattered. So how's your book?"

Henry caresses the cover. "As good as it was the last five times. Davies has the stuff."

"That's my last name!" I say. "I wonder if we're related. I should read it."

"You may not be old enough for him yet."

"Why? Is he filthy?" Meryl asks.

Henry laughs. "Risqué, from time to time, but not filthy."

"What does he write about?"

"Well, this one, or I should say these three, are about . . . oh, lots of things, but perhaps mostly about guilt: people who feel it but shouldn't, people who should but don't. And also what it means to live in the shadow of a strong father, and what it is to have wasted your potential. Or to only look like you have."

"What does he think is the difference?" I ask.

"I'm not sure that's a question Davies wants to answer. I

think for his characters, it depends somewhat on who's watching—and judging."

"Deep," Meryl says. "God, I'm exhausted. I'm going to bed. You coming?" She pokes me in the ribs.

"In a minute. Henry, when you finish, can I borrow that?"

Henry nods. "I'll be interested to hear what you think of it."

There are two zippers on the tent flap, and I fumble for a few minutes before I figure out how to unzip them both. I crawl in. It's a small tent. Is Meryl already asleep?

"I lied," Meryl says.

"What about?"

"I'm not exhausted."

Again she takes charge, and something about it bothers me, so I pin her arms and wrestle her until I'm on top, but she just laughs like that's what she intended all along, and melts underneath me like icing.

Afterward I can't make myself fall asleep, even when the tent warms and I can see daylight through the blue fabric.

I wonder where Nick went. I wonder if Henry, or anyone, believes the bear story. Maybe Nick reported the thefts to the ranger. It's easy to imagine him doing it.

He'd be so sincere.

"HEY. YOU SNORE." Meryl pokes me in the ribs. "And also it's, like, noon."

"Sorry."

"S'okay. It's kinda cute." She rumples my hair, then pushes her own out of her eyes. "God. What am I doing?"

"Telling me to wake up, I thought."

Meryl snickers. "Right. That's it. Okay then. Wake up."

She sits on my stomach and starts to tickle me.

"I'm not ticklish."

"Bullshit, everyone's ticklish."

"Nope," I say, staying perfectly still as Meryl keeps on trying. "Not me. Sorry. But you know, there are *some* people— you don't even have to touch them to tickle them. Like for instance I could say, 'Behind your left knee,' and suddenly the area behind your left knee would be *so* ticklish."

Meryl clutches her left knee. "Agh! Stop it! How are you *doing* that?"

I push Meryl off my stomach and sit up. "In the curve of your right elbow."

Meryl is helpless with laughter. "Stop stop stop, oh my God, stop!"

"Stop what? The back of your neck."

Meryl wheezes, grabbing her neck as though she's about to strangle herself. "No fair!"

"Hey!" It's Nick, outside the tent. "Everybody okay in there?" He sounds amused.

"Don't put yourself out on our account. We're just fine," Meryl says.

"Actually I have to get up," I say softly. I grab my toothbrush, toothpaste, soap, and a towel, climb over Meryl, unzip the tent flap, and step out into the sun.

"I hear you went looking for us last night," I say to Nick, who's lying on Aurora's camp sofa. "To protect us from the marauding bears. We didn't see any, by the way."

THE WOMEN'S RESTROOM has showers at one end, like a gym. Annalisa's doing yoga stretches as she stands under the water, and Aurora has bright green cream smeared all over her face and neck.

"Good morning!" Annalisa says. "I'm glad you made it back all right. It must've been after I fell asleep. We thought you might have gotten lost."

"No. We were just down at the beach."

"Is it gorgeous?" Aurora asks. "Your brother and I were talking about getting everyone to go for a swim later."

"It's nice."

"But will the beach be thronged? That's what I'm afraid of," Annalisa says.

"It wasn't bad last night when Meryl and I were there."

"I'm *so* glad the two of you are getting to be friends!" Aurora says. "It's hard when you move into a house where everyone knows each other already and you're the odd girl out."

"Oh, you're living with Aurora, too?" Annalisa asks, beginning to towel herself dry. "I didn't realize you'd been indoctrinated into the cult."

"Annalisa, please! Forest House is not a cult! And if there *were* a cult leader in training among our acquaintances, I assure you it would not be me. My powers of persuasion are *quite* limited." Aurora uses a washcloth to wipe off her green cream.

I hope Nick's never considered that as a career choice.

When we go down to the beach later, Meryl rubs waterproof sunscreen into all the places I can't reach.

"Boys all over America would pay good money to see that," Damian says. "Not to mention some girls."

"God, shut up, Damian," Meryl says.

"What? I speak only the truth. Lesbianism: it's the palatable deviance. As opposed to the terrifying specter of male homosexuality." He bats his eyelashes.

Meryl abandons me to chase Damian into the ocean. In doing so, she loses her balance and falls into the shallow water close to the shore. She and Damian splash and try to duck each other, cackling madly.

I shield my eyes from the sun's glare. Damian and Meryl are still splashing and laughing. Aurora and Annalisa are lying on their stomachs—Annalisa's reading a fashion magazine; Aurora's going over her blue notebook. Nick had decided to swim all the way out to the buoy, and he's about halfway back. I can just see him if I squint. Robert's crouched close to the water's edge, taking close-up pictures with his digital camera of the patterns the waves have made in the sand. Charles is watching a crab. Henry's asleep, a towel over his face, his book resting on his bare, hairy chest. If he naps long enough, he'll get a damn funny-looking tan line.

Now Damian's giving Meryl a piggyback ride. She's hanging on him and whispering into his ear.

I'll cop to being kind of a ho.

Nick surfaces, close to shore. He walks up to me and shakes himself like a dog. I jump away, but the drops of water feel nice, like when you run through a sprinkler.

"Hey, whatcha thinking? Isn't it fantastic here? This was such a great idea, don't you think?"

"Yeah, sure."

"We're in an absolutely amazing place, in great company, we're young, and the sun is shining!"

I sigh.

Nick puts a wet arm around me.

"Is something wrong? What's going on?"

There are so many things I could say.

"Nothing ever gets to you," I mumble.

Nick squeezes my shoulders, then lets go. "It's called *acting*. Come on, young lady, what you need is total immersion." And he drags me down to the water, which is freezing, possibly literally.

We run into Meryl and Damian, and whatever they were doing underwater turns into a free-for-all, everyone splashing everyone else, all four of us ducking each other under, grabbing whichever limb is closest, everyone cracking up. Even me, until the salt water goes up my nose and I start to cough. Then I decide it's time to get out of the water and let myself dry off in the sun. I lay out my towel next to Annalisa's and Aurora's, just as Annalisa's asking, "When are you going to tell them?"

Aurora shakes her head and glances in my direction. "A lot still needs to be worked out. And besides, *that* part doesn't need to happen overnight. Unlike the ceremony."

That part?

"Yes, but I bet Robert wants it to happen sooner rather than later. You two have been out of college for a while, you know."

"You're not wrong. But first things first. Our insane costume wedding!"

"I still can't believe it—I'm so happy for you! And I'm *thrilled* about the costume idea—it's sheer genius. I know exactly what I'm going to wear. But you and Robert, married—don't take this the wrong way, but how did you *know*?"

"You mean aside from the nice letter from the INS?" Aurora asks.

"Yes."

Aurora says, "I'll be brutally honest with you, Annalisa.

I think the letter helped. I told you he'd already proposed, weeks and weeks ago, didn't I?"

Annalisa shakes her head. "I had no idea."

Aurora continues, "Well, I . . . I actually got quite *incensed* when he proposed, just because of the timing, and I told him I couldn't possibly make a major decision like that until after the show closed." She laughs. "But then"—her voice gets softer—"the letter came, and it forced me to think about what it would be like if he had to move back to Canada. And it was *terrifying*, just to contemplate it. I mean, for so *many* reasons. Annalisa, I know myself. I'm not one for false modesty. There's a lot that I'm good at. But I'm very *bad* at seeing when I'm pushing things too far, when I'm overextending, when it's time to stop."

"I hear you," Annalisa says. "I have that problem myself. With the Ghirardelli, among other things." She sighs, and pinches the roll of flesh at her hips. "Sometimes I think the trouble with me and Paul—that's Ellery's dad, I think you've met him—was that we were too much alike."

Aurora nods, and goes on. "Anyway, when I'm going over the edge, Robert always sees it before I do. It's like he catches me *before* I fall."

Aurora shades her eyes to smile out at Robert, still squatting on the sand with his camera. His stomach spills out over his swimming trunks, and he does not look like a vision of romance, to say the least. I wonder when, and how, she decided that what she has with him trumped the thrill of being with someone new.

"You can just stop now," Annalisa says. "If you keep going like that I'll have to either kill you or cry. I can't believe I have to be *out* there again. And, of course, it doesn't help that Ellery finds it supremely disgusting to contemplate her mother dating."

"Of course. The young always do. No offense, Battle."

"I'm a little older than Ellery," I say.

Aurora and Annalisa laugh.

WHEN WE'RE ALL walking back to the campsite before dinner, Meryl pulls me aside. "Look," she says in an undertone, "we're clear, right?"

"About?"

"You know."

"I'm not sure."

Meryl sighs and lights a cigarette.

I wonder where she got them. Maybe she's had them all along.

"Well," Meryl says, "you know I'm older than you. I'm twenty-two. And I get the idea I'm, oh, maybe just a little more experienced with certain things. But you're obviously smart, so I'm sure you know that sometimes things happen and it's really nice, but it doesn't have to be a big deal. Not everything's super deep and meaningful, right? There's this thing of friends with benefits—you know what I mean, right?"

"Then why don't you just not *talk* about it?"

I walk faster, but Meryl matches my pace.

"Well, I didn't want you to, you know, get the wrong idea. I mean that's so often the problem when you hook up with girls, it's like suddenly they think you're engaged or something, and also, like I said before, we're housemates, so it'd be a bad idea for things to continue."

"Right. Because that's always stopped you before."

IT'S HENRY'S JOB to make dinner tonight, and he does it not by cooking anything but instead by laying out an elaborate spread of foods that do not require any preparation: meats, cheeses, loaves of bread, mixed nuts, crackers, red and green grapes, apples, strawberries, raspberries, and blueberries, and, of course, several kinds of chocolate. For a while, he and I are the only ones awake to eat it, everyone else having retreated to their various tents to nap.

"Ah, they're all sun-punished," Henry says through a mouthful of grapes. "I'm surprised that you're not sleeping with the rest of them."

"I'm not even sleeping with one of them," I say, and Henry laughs his loud, carrying laugh.

"Really? Should I congratulate you, or commiserate?"

"I don't know."

"Then I'll just nod wisely," says Henry, doing so.

"What are you going to wear to the wedding?" I ask.

"Well, I hadn't really thought about it. I'd enjoy the donkey's ears, but it might set the wrong tone."

"Charles said we're not allowed to use *Dream* costumes, anyway, remember?"

He'd announced at rehearsal that the *Dream* costumes were "verboten." "Any of the rest of them, though, are up for grabs. Just don't spill anything on yourself, avoid infusing the costumes with bodily fluids, and if all else fails, remember that the profession of dry cleaner is a noble one, worthy of your patronage."

"Oh, that's right," Henry says. "Charles is a smart man. Well, what would you recommend, Miss B?"

"Hmm. I guess Friar Lawrence would be a little obvious."

"Not to mention ominous! But never mind, I'm sure something will come to me. What about you?"

"I don't know, either," I say, but as soon as I've said it, I get an idea, and decide not to tell Henry, or anyone.

Henry and I eat and drink in silence for a while, and then people begin crawling out of their tents. I'm not interested in interacting with anyone else now, so I ask Henry, "Are you done with that book? I'd still like to borrow it, if that's okay."

It is. I take the book, along with his headlamp, some

chocolate, and a bottle of Damian's wine, and walk down to the beach by myself to read. The book is a little hard to follow, especially after I've been drinking for a while. But I do understand that at the beginning, one boy threw a snowball with a stone in it at another boy. It didn't hit him. It hit a pregnant woman, and her baby was born prematurely, and then she went crazy.

But it's not the boy who threw the stone who feels guilty. It's the other one.

He blames himself for ducking.

Later, my head spinning, I find out how much space two people can create between them in a small tent when they don't want to touch.

scene ii

BACK IN PORTLAND, I stalk Reed. Between work and rehearsals, I pace the campus, read the online communities (full of references and in-jokes that make no sense, yet), learn the names of buildings and professors. Trying to get a handle on the near future is a good distraction from the present.

Then one day Robert shows up at rehearsal to beg for help in the scene shop. I jump at this further opportunity to escape from Forest House.

When I played Rosalind back in high school, I avoided the scene shop because it was demented: toxic half-full cans of paint, boards with old nails sticking out, rusty coffee cans of nuts and washers that people were always knocking over, and a table saw that everyone said had separated at least one technician from his index finger.

But when I walk into Robert's scene shop, I breathe in the clean new-wood scent of a hardware store. Everything— wood, nails, screws, bolts, nuts, washers, paint, glue, fabric— is stored in clearly labeled, logically placed storage boxes, shelves, drawers, and bins. Now I understand his clipboard at the campsite.

Nic would love this place.

We still IM a lot, along with our other friends from that summer, Katrina and Isaac. Katrina and Isaac also started seeing each other while we were all at the Siegel Institute. They're still trying, despite the fact that they live even farther away from each other than Nic and I do. Every so often Isaac forwards Nic and me a long, drawn-out e-mail from Katrina where she's taking him to task about some minutely detailed combination of relationship issues, and asks for our advice on how to respond.

Nic's much better at that than I am.

Which was always part of the problem.

Most of the time, I don't know why *I* do things—or don't do them—let alone what motivates anyone else.

As Nic never failed to point out.

If Nic was in my current situation, she'd demand to have a long talk with Meryl about what happened on the camping trip, and before that, at the gun range, and exactly what it means. I can't imagine what she'd do if she had a brother like Nick, but I'm sure it would also involve some kind of prolonged, overly analytical conversation.

Damn, I miss her.

A guy steps from behind one of the shelving units, making me jump.

"Can I help you?"

"Robert said you guys needed people?"

He sizes me up. "You're not exactly dressed for it—we're repainting the night sky."

"I don't mind," I say, though he's right that my white T-shirt isn't a stellar choice.

"Follow me, then."

We go into the next room, where there's a huge curtain laid out on the floor. The curtain has lots of holes. Several people, Robert among them, are sitting or sprawling on it, painting.

"Hey," I say to the group. Then, to Robert, "Are we going to sew up the holes, too?"

"Those aren't holes," a girl says. "Those are the stars."

"There'll be light shining through from behind," Robert explains.

"Oh, cool!"

"We're glad you think so," the guy I saw first says. He sounds like he means the opposite, so I grab a brush, stake out a section of curtain, and shut up.

It's obvious that the others have known each other for a long time. Their conversation, I realize gradually, consists in equal parts of quotes from movies and utterly incomprehensible in-jokes. They call Robert "Fearless Leader," or sometimes "Leerless Feeder," and refer to themselves as the Minions. Just when I've decided to tune out the conversation, one of the Minions asks, "So is that one brunette with the rack in this show?"

"Jesus, I hope so. She's really *friendly*," says another.

"Friends with benefits!" says a third.

I feel hot all over.

"Yeah, dude, she's got so many friends with benefits, she could, like, start her own retirement plan."

"That's not what I heard."

"Well, obviously, she wouldn't give *you* the time of day."

"Who says I'd want it from her?"

"We know what you want."

I don't need to hear this.

"Who cares about her? Is tall, blond, and hung going to grace us with his presence?"

I *really* don't need to hear this.

"Dude, you do know that's his sister, right?" a girl I've never met says, and I wonder how she knows.

"Oops, sorry. TMI, huh?"

I manage to smile and nod.

The Minions shift to more mundane subjects: the chances that the roof will start leaking again before the show goes up, the relative merits of duct tape and electrical tape, whether slow zombie or fast zombie movies are superior.

When we stop, my T-shirt is almost as blue as my jeans, and my arms and back are sore.

"You look wiped," Meryl says from the sofa when I walk into Forest House.

"I was helping Robert and, uh, the Minions."

"Oh, yeah, I totally forgot that was tonight. Not that I was gonna go—they're all such horndogs!—did you get sexually harrassed?"

"No. Mostly they talked about zombies."

"And you were painting, I see. C'mere, you have some blue on your face."

I kneel beside the couch. She licks her index finger and rubs it hard on my forehead.

"There, that's got it."

"Thanks, Mom."

I move so that I'm leaning against the couch.

"Aw, you're so exhausted. I'll give you a backrub."

I guess this is part of my benefit package.

scene iii

I'M IN MY car, halfway to rehearsal, when I see a dog—a little beige mop of a dog, running back and forth across the street, darting between speeding cars. He has no leash, no collar, and there's no one in sight who looks like they have any connection with him.

I slam on the brakes, get out of the car, run over to the dog, and scoop him up into my arms.

"Are you lost? What were you thinking, little moron? Little stupid dog, what were you doing in the street, huh?"

Horns honk, reminding me that I've left the car stopped in the middle of the road with the driver's-side door wide open.

I get back in, pull over, and sit with the dog on my lap until my heartbeat slows. The dog is calm. He doesn't run around inside the car, he doesn't shake, he doesn't bark once. I stroke his head and he wags his tail.

"You're lucky," I tell him. "You are so lucky. Yes, that's what you are. Lucky. Hey, Lucky. Hey good dog, sweet dog, Lucky."

Lucky looks up at me. He has the kind of doggy face that makes him look like he's smiling. I pet his head and he licks my hand.

"Okay, Lucky, now I have to get to rehearsal, but don't

worry, I'm not going to abandon you—I'm going to take you inside with me, okay?"

Lucky blinks.

I pet him some more, then start the car again and pull out into the traffic. It's hard to concentrate on driving. I stomp hard on the brakes to avoid running into the sport utility vehicle in front of me. Lucky doesn't react.

"Sorry, sweetie. You're so good! Such a good little quiet one."

"WHERE HAVE YOU been?" asks Aurora. "And what is *that*?"

Rehearsal's been under way for half an hour by the time Lucky and I make it to the theater.

"I'm sorry I'm late, but look—he was out in the street, there was no one—he was going to get run over any minute—I had to take him, and then I didn't want him to run again, so I picked up a collar and a leash."

"Oh." Aurora softens. "Ah, look at this little sweetheart. I don't know if animals are technically allowed in the building, but we can make a onetime exception, don't you think so?" She addresses this question to Lucky, and answers it a moment later, scratching him under the chin. "Yes, I think so, oh yes, we'll be making an exception for you."

"And there *is* a dog in the show," I point out. "We could just say that this is Moon's dog, right?"

"You shouldn't have picked him up," Nick says. "He obviously belongs to someone—look what good shape he's in. You just stole somebody's *dog*."

"He was running back and forth across a really busy street. Nobody around looked like they cared. I didn't want to *steal* him, I just didn't want him to *die* in front of me, okay?"

"Were you pissed?" Meryl asks. "I would have been. God, I can't stand it when people let their dogs run around off leash; it's not like we're out in the country or something."

"There was no one to be pissed *at*; that was the point."

Nick looks at Aurora. "Can we get back to where we were?"

Robert and the Minions are in the scene shop again, still painting, so I leave Lucky with them for the rest of rehearsal.

"Seems like a sweet little guy," one of the Minions says when I come in to retrieve him. "But he was kind of a pain—started crying as soon as you left, and he didn't stop till just now."

"Oh, I'm so sorry." I kneel to pet Lucky. Thinking about him crying because I was gone makes me feel like my heart might shatter. "You're okay," I tell him. "You're fine."

Nick and Meryl have followed me into the scene shop. Nick says, "Look, you have to take this dog back where he belongs."

"He didn't have a collar."

"He probably has a microchip. We'll get him to a vet with a scanner," Nick says, glaring at Lucky.

"Maybe he ran away for a reason," I say, not looking at Nick.

"Oh, I'm sure he considered it very carefully. Brain the size of a walnut. You're taking him to the vet, it's not optional."

Does Nick think I can't take care of a dog? But he knows about Dante and Beatrice.

"Come on, Lucky," I say, standing up. "Let's take you outside."

Meryl walks close behind me. "You've *named* the dog? Not a good idea. You shouldn't get too attached."

Too late. "He's a really good dog."

Lucky lifts his leg and pees on a rosemary bush.

"Yeah, looks like he's pretty talented," Meryl says.

I WALK INTO Forest House holding Lucky. Nick and Meryl are behind me. Aurora and Robert went for a late dinner alone, to go over the wedding plans. The wedding, and, of course, the show, are coming up frighteningly soon.

Charles looks up from watering one of the African violets and sneezes. "Is that a dog? I'm sorry, I'm allergic," he says. "Please don't bring it into the house."

"I'm just going to take him up to my room. If I leave him outside, he'll cry."

"Why do you have a dog?"

"I found him. In traffic. He's Lucky."

"Doesn't sound lucky," Charles says.

"Lucky not to've been flattened," Meryl says.

"Lucky that my sucker of a sister grabbed him up out of the path of the oncoming semi, saving him from certain death," Nick says.

"He wasn't in the path of a semi," I say.

"Oh. Well, God, it hardly seems like there was much of a threat, then."

Charles sneezes again, rubs his eyes. "I'm sorry, but could you please put the dog outside?"

"I can't leave him alone."

"I guess you'll have to stay outside with him, then," Nick says.

"Fine," I say.

The night is cool and clear. I set up my sleeping bag on the back porch. I rub Lucky behind his floppy ears, then spend several minutes combing a mat out of his fur with my fingers, staring out at the garden as I do it. All the white flowers look like little ghosts in the dark.

"Hey," Meryl says from behind me. I hear the click of her lighter. "Doing real well not getting attached, I see."

"And you're doing really well not smoking."

"Oh, you know. I've been helping Aurora a lot with all the wedding crap and you may not have noticed, but she's totally on edge. There's always *one more thing* that's somehow messed up. And it's not like she thinks I can *fix* any of the idiotic problems, but I'm supposed to be just as obsessed about it as she is."

"So *you're* smoking because *Aurora's* stressed out?"

Meryl shrugs.

Lucky barks once.

"Lucky," I say, and he's quiet again.

"I can't believe you named him."

I raise myself onto my elbows. "You have to call a dog something."

Meryl exhales a small, smoky cloud. "He's not yours."

"Maybe he will be."

Meryl shakes her head. "Sweetie, you can't have a dog."

"Why not, Mom? I promise I'll take good care of him."

"Time. Money."

"I have enough." I'm not sure if I mean money or time.

"Oh, right, you've got a monster trust fund, I forgot. I guess you can just get the dog his own apartment, then."

"I do not have a monster trust fund. Jesus."

Meryl sits down next to me. "So how are you paying your rent? Not to mention getting people's trucks fixed. I know how much canvassers make."

"Why do you care?" I ask.

And then I'm crying.

Lucky puts his head in my lap and I scratch behind his ears.

"He really likes you," Meryl says. Her voice is softer. Because she can see me crying? "You're good with him."

"That's because I *have* dogs. Two. I had to leave them with Mom and Dad. *They* probably *are* in a damn apartment. A kennel, anyway."

"Ugh."

"Yeah. When I go back there to visit, I doubt they'll even remember me."

Meryl moves even closer. She stubs out her cigarette and tosses it into an empty flowerpot. Then she uses her index finger to trace a line from my cheekbone to my chin.

"You're pretty memorable."

I slap her hand away. "Stop it."

"What?"

"Just stop it. It's stupid."

"What's stupid?"

"You were going to kiss me again."

Meryl looks away. "How do you know what I was going to do?"

"You had that look. And you know, it would've been fine. I would've liked it. But guess what? In an hour, or a day, or a week, you'd say, 'Oh, no, sorry, you're going to make a big deal out of this, you're not going to be able to handle it.' I'm tired of it. You just go back inside. I'll stay out here with my dog. Who isn't mine."

Meryl stands up. She looks for a minute as though she's going to say something. But then she just takes another cigarette out of her pack, sticks it into her mouth, lights it, and walks away.

I can't seem to stop crying. Lucky licks my face. He has bad breath.

"Here," Nick says. He tosses a box of dog treats at me. "For the mutt."

"So, where'd you get it?" I wipe my eyes. "Did you mug somebody? Was a car door conveniently unlocked?"

"Hey. None of that. These are straight from Posh Pets. They're high quality, all organic and whole grain." He picks up the box, rips it open, and pops a treat into his own mouth.

He spits it out a second later. Lucky goes onto his hind legs and catches it midair.

"Good dog!" I laugh and applaud.

"Blech. I'm not doing that again," Nick says. He spits again.

"I'm sure he'll eat another one, even if it doesn't have the special saliva coating." I reach into the box and hold out another treat. Lucky crunches it.

"There's a twenty-four-hour emergency vet across town," Nick says. "I just called to make sure she has the scanner, and she does. We should take him now."

I put my face in my hands and rub away more traces of

tears. "Sure. Why not? I've been having such a great night anyway."

I give Lucky one more treat. Then I hug him, which almost makes me start to cry again.

At the vet's, everyone in the waiting room looks as sad as I do, and that makes me feel worse. They all have histories with their hurt, sick, and dying animals, years and years together. I haven't even had one day, and still I feel like I won't be able to stand it, letting Lucky go.

"You should feel good," Nick says, nudging me. "You're gonna get this little guy back home."

"Why are you being *nice*?" I snap. "I thought you didn't even think he was worth getting out of the path of a *semi*."

"Ah, you know, I wasn't really mad at the dog," Nick says. He scratches Lucky behind the ears. "It's just, I've lived here longer than you have. You see dogs running around off leash constantly. I was mad that you were putting yourself out because someone else was being irresponsible."

I look at my brother, considering several possible responses to what he's just said.

"Davies?" the vet calls. So I say nothing, just take Lucky into the little examining room.

It smells like fur and disinfectant. The wand-shaped scanner is like the ones from stores, except that it doesn't beep after the scanning's done.

If only it meant I'd just bought him.

"Okay," the vet says. "I've got the owner's phone number, but for privacy reasons, I can't share it with you. But if you can wait a while longer, I'll have someone call. I'm sure they'll want him back as soon as possible. They may want to meet you here, or sometimes owners don't mind giving out their address and you can just take him right back home. Good for you, bringing him in. It's a nice change to see such a healthy little guy."

She rubs Lucky's belly, then walks out, closing the door behind her.

LUCKY'S HOUSE TURNS out to be less than a mile from the busy street where I found him. It's a small brown house, and the porch light is on.

The driveway is clear, but I park on the street, several houses away. Then I can't make myself get out of the car. I lift Lucky out of Nick's lap and hug him one more time. He licks my face again, oblivious.

"Here," I say, handing him back to Nick, "I can't do this part."

Nick nods. "Be right back."

An eternity later, he opens the passenger door and gets back into the car, without saying anything.

"So, were they happy?" I ask finally.

"You really want to know?"

"Yes. Otherwise I wouldn't have asked."

"The woman who opened the door looked tired," Nick says. "I handed her the dog and told her that we'd found him out in traffic, and she just sort of nodded and said, 'Yeah, he's a runner.'"

"Fuck. Can we go back in there and get him?"

"Don't worry. It got better. There was a little boy behind her, and as soon as he saw the dog, he started jumping up and down and saying, 'It's Baby! It's Baby! He's back! It's Baby!'"

I let out my breath in a long sigh. "Okay. He'll probably be right back out there on the damn street tomorrow, but okay."

Nick squeezes my shoulder. "You did the right thing."

I'm beginning to think the *right* thing would've been for me to stay in Chapel Hill, have a boring, frustrating summer, and wait until orientation started to shake up my life. At least then I'd have been with *my* dogs.

scene iv

IT'S OUR FIRST run-through with all the tech cues in place.

Aurora and Robert are getting married tomorrow.

And Nick's missing.

We wait for him for forty-five minutes before we get going,

but he never shows. Aurora has to read his lines. She's livid, then frantic.

"He *must* have said something to you about where he was going to be," she says to me when we're back at Forest House and he still hasn't turned up. "This is completely unlike him."

It's exactly like him.

"I have no idea where he is. I have no idea when he'll be back. He doesn't tell me things like that," I say.

"But aren't you *worried*? We don't know what could have happened to him!"

"I didn't know what had happened to him for years," I mutter, too softly for anyone to hear.

"*I'm* worried," Charles says in a low voice.

"Is anyone else *pissed*?" Meryl demands. "He wasted everyone's time tonight. Anyone else remember how he said that he wasn't sure he wanted the part? What if he's just suddenly decided to leave the show at the last minute?"

The wind outside gets loud, and sheets of rain begin splattering down. I shiver. It feels as though the temperature's just dropped ten degrees.

"He wouldn't do that. No, something must have happened, and now he's out in this storm. . . ." Aurora walks to the living-room window and peers out as though she thinks at any moment a bedraggled Nick will push open the gate. The trees sway, the gate creaks, torrents of water fall from the sky.

I call Nick. I called him at rehearsal, too. He didn't pick up then, and I don't expect him to now. He doesn't. I listen to his message again: "Hey, it's Nick. I can't talk right now, but I'm *so* glad you called! Leave me a message and I'll get back to you as soon as I can."

"Where the hell are you? Everyone's worried. Stay dry and call me back."

I shut the phone and survey the room. Aurora has decided that the level of her worry for Nick warrants a drink, and she's pouring bourbon into an ice-filled glass. Meryl has stalked out onto the porch and is trying, and failing, to light a cigarette in the driving rain. Charles is pinching dead leaves off one of the rubber trees, the way someone else might have cracked his knuckles or bitten her nails. Robert, predictably, is the only one unaffected. He's sitting in the battered green armchair, his legs propped on the coffee table, reading a book called *Perfect Circle*, looking content.

I go out onto the porch. The wind is whipping Meryl's hair around her face. She's given up for the moment on lighting the cigarette, but it still dangles from her lips, and she continues to hold her lighter.

"He's a fucker," she says. "He's a thoughtless bastard."

Exactly. But I say, "You don't know what happened. He could be hurt."

Meryl laughs a short, barking laugh that knocks the cigarette out of her mouth.

"It won't be anything bad. He's like a goddamn cat. You could fling him off the side of the Empire State Building and he'd land on his feet. Probably collect some money from passersby while he was at it. You know. Nice little impromptu performance."

"Shut up." But I can see it in my mind: the fall, like a dive. The way he'd spin in the air, just before impact. The graceful landing. The smile. The bow.

Meryl stares into the rain. "I can't imagine being related to him."

"Imagine not being a bitch," I say. Then I go back inside.

It's startlingly dark.

"Power just went out," Robert says. "Aurora's looking for candles."

"I'll look, too," I say. "I think Nick might have some left from the camping trip."

I see another of Meryl's lighters on the coffee table and flick it into flame.

I climb the stairs, slowly to avoid the flowerpots, and stand in front of Nick's door. It's slightly ajar, so it doesn't feel quite so much like an invasion of privacy to push it the rest of the way open.

I don't really think there'll be any candles inside. I'm not sure what I'm looking for. What he stole from the mansion, maybe? Other, unknown objects he's taken from other places?

It's just a stark, unornamented space, with a futon on the floor, a gym mat, the blue plaid armchair, a dresser, some garbage bags full of laundry—it reveals nothing. Maybe there'll be something inside the dresser. I pull open the top drawer. Underwear and an open box of condoms. The ones from the camping trip? Ugh, I don't want to know.

The second drawer is more interesting. It contains, on top of a collection of T-shirts, the photo album I gave him, and programs for the last few shows he's been in. I pick up the one from *The Taming of the Shrew*, feeling a little queasy, and hold it up to the lighter—not too close, so I don't set it on fire. On the front is a photo of Nick, in doublet and hose, with Meryl, in a froth of skirts and petticoats, bent over his knee. Nick's hand is raised, the picture capturing the moment before he spanks her.

I put the program back. The rest of the drawers hold nothing but clothes.

I open the closet door. There are a few shirts and a jacket hanging up. I feel in the pockets of the jacket. God, what am I looking for—a gun? No, that would be in Meryl's closet, if it were anywhere.

There's no gun, of course.

But the small green thing that he stole from the mansion—it's a box of some kind, maybe to hold letters, but with nothing in it—is there.

I put the small green box in my own pocket.

There's also an envelope. Again, I hold it close to the lighter's flame so I can see what it is.

A bill.

FINAL NOTICE is printed on it, in red. It's unopened.

Then I look down and see that the floor of the closet is littered with similar envelopes, an inch or so deep.

So, several months worth, at least. I kneel, pick up a handful, and feel along the flap of each envelope.

None of them have been opened.

Many of them have similarly worded red-ink warnings.

"Nick collects for utilities," I remember Charles telling me.

Collects, but doesn't pay, apparently.

There are credit card bills, too.

I let the envelopes fall from my hands, then sit cross-legged on Nick's gym mat in the dark and listen for a while to the rain. It's still coming down hard and fast. It sounds as though, if you were outside in it, each drop would sting your skin.

Then I hear the front door open, and I run down the stairs just in time to see Nick walk through the door and take in the fact that the power's gone out.

"Oh, no," he says to the room at large. "Downed power

lines, huh? God, it's brutal out—batten down the hatches, people. I've *never* seen a storm like this in Portland."

Downed power lines. Right.

I guess it *could* be.

"Where were you? Are you okay?" Aurora cries, half-angry, half-worried.

"Oh, yeah, I'm fine. And hey, I'm glad *you* guys are all home. It's so nasty out there," he says.

"We'd all like to know where you were," Robert says.

Charles, who was out of the room, comes back in with a box of candles. He hands one to each of us, takes one for himself, lights it, then goes around and lights ours with his. Once all the candles are lit—was he waiting for atmospheric lighting?—Nick sighs, and says, "Well, y'all, what happened was ugly. I was on the train on the way to rehearsal, and there was an accident. The train collided with an ambulance. It was really, really bad. And anyway, those of us on the train had to stay there until the police had come and talked to us, and the paramedics had to look us over to make sure we didn't have concussions or anything."

"But I called you. I called you *twice*," I say.

"I don't doubt it. And I would've answered—hell, I wanted to call *you*—but the damn charge gave out on my worthless phone."

The graceful landing, the smile, the bow.

"*Are* you okay?" I hear myself ask.

"Haven't noticed any whiplash yet."

A drop splashes from the candle onto the back of my hand. It hurts, but only for a moment. Then I peel it off, roll it into a tiny ball, and push it back into the soft wax closest to the flame.

If we had power, I could check his story on the local news or online.

But we don't, of course.

"So—anyone for hearts by candlelight?" Nick asks.

"At least two of us need to make it an early night. Big day tomorrow," says Robert. Aurora smiles, and they go upstairs together.

"We can do one game," Charles says, "but then we should all get to sleep. Think of tomorrow as a performance. Just not of the show."

We play in the kitchen, so the cards get smeared with the ice cream we're gorging ourselves with before it melts. And despite Charles's reminder, Meryl's decided that tonight, hearts is a drinking game.

I can't focus. Not because I'm drinking—I don't feel like impairing my judgment any further than it already is. I keep wondering if Nick will notice, later, that I've been in his room. And that I've stolen the box he stole.

When I'm not glancing nervously at my brother, I can't

stop looking at Meryl. She keeps leaning over the table when she puts down a card, and her halter's coverage is minimal, to say the least. I imagine letting the Dulce de Leche slide off my spoon into her cleavage. If my brother and Charles weren't in the room, I'd do it.

Eventually, Meryl shoots the moon and does one more shot of bourbon, then bids everyone good night and heads upstairs, carrying a candle with stiff dignity, like a girl from some earlier century.

What if she falls asleep without blowing it out and starts a fire in her room?

"She was pretty drunk," I say to the room at large. "I'd better check on her."

"Oh, is that what the kids are calling it these days?" Nick asks with a knowing smile.

"Shut up," I say, and go up to her room.

I came out to Nick soon after he found me, on the theory that if he was going to freak, I wanted it to happen before I got used to having him back in my life. His reaction: "Guess we're both out of the will, then, huh?"

I open Meryl's door and breathe in a mixture of chlorine, tobacco, and sandalwood incense. It's dark, so she did remember to blow out the candle. When my eyes adjust, I discover that, like Pippi Longstocking, Meryl sleeps backward. Her feet are pointed at the headboard, resting on the pillow, and the rest of her is invisible underneath a thick black comforter.

I pick my way through the mess on Meryl's floor, kick off my shoes, and climb into bed next to her.

Meryl's breathing just fine. She's fallen asleep in her clothes, and she's slightly overheated. Being next to her is a little like curling up with a large cat.

"Fancy meeting you here," Meryl says, muffled.

"I was making sure you didn't die of alcohol poisoning. Or set your room on fire."

"Really?" Meryl blinks and stretches. "Gosh. I feel fine."

"I was worried."

Then I kiss her, and sure, maybe it's because I'm trying not to think about my brother, but I don't care, it's sweet. And when she pulls off her shirt, and then mine, and presses herself against me, it's even sweeter.

IN THE MIDDLE of the night, I'm suddenly awake, and for the second before I hear Meryl's breathing, I'm not sure where I am. Then I remember, and look over at her. She's sleeping soundly, and I'm glad. She doesn't stir when I slide out from underneath the coverlet, retrieve my scattered clothing, get dressed, and creep back to my own room.

WHEN I WAKE up, a glance at the dark display of my digital clock confirms that the power's still out. I sigh and rub my eyes. My hands smell like Meryl, and thinking about that part of last night makes me feel like I went to the circus and ate a lot of cotton candy, and now the sugar's making my teeth ache.

Then I'm visualizing the bills on Nick's floor again. I try to summon up anger, disgust, outrage, but none of them come. Instead, there's just a dullness. I'd like to pull the covers over my head and sleep through the day, but I can't.

I have a wedding to attend.

When I was little, weddings were Dad's excuse for never taking us on vacation. Every weekend, June through August, Dad pronounced some couple husband and wife, and wished them lifelong happiness. As I got older, I found this increasingly ironic. It was one of the many reasons I was glad when he and Mom decided to start sending me away in the summers.

But I haven't *been* to a wedding in years. The last one I can remember going to was when this friend of Mom's from church, Marybeth, got remarried to a balding mortgage broker named Gary. The ceremony was earnest and endless, and there was a lot of overwrought music and talk about second chances.

I guess this one is going to be about second chances, too—or maybe third or fourth or tenth. Aside from the thing with Henry, I'm not clear on the details of Aurora's romantic past.

It seems improbable that it would be anything other than the first and only chance for Robert, but the other day, I overheard him talking with the Minions about an ex. "After Fran," he said, "my back and my credit rating never recovered." The Minions pressed him for details, especially about the sexual escapades that they assumed had put his back out of commission, but he refused to provide any.

I hear the water running—someone's beaten me into the shower. Probably Charles, who tends to be the earliest riser in the house. While I wait, I contemplate my costume. I thought of it while we were on the camping trip, and even then, I knew it was a little strange. Now I wish I'd picked anything else, but there's no time to come up with a different concept.

The water stops, and I head down the hall to the bathroom, passing Charles, who's wrapped in a towel.

"That your costume?" I ask.

"Absolutely," he says.

We smile at each other, and I go in to take my shower.

I flick the light switch automatically. The power's still out. I don't know why I thought it would be back on. At least some light comes in through the window.

Then, as always in Forest House, I marvel at how many hygiene-related products a house full of people can accumulate, and how much everyone manages to shed. I pull a tangled, multihued hairball out of the drain, feeling vaguely ill, and toss it into the already-overflowing wastebasket. Since rehearsals have gotten into full swing, chores have mostly fallen by the wayside. I'm looking forward to being in the dorm, when I will have only one roommate. Once school starts, I have no idea how often I'll see anyone from Forest House.

Including Nick.

I turn off the water, wrap myself in the last clean dry towel, and make it back to my room with no housemate encounters. I'm hoping I won't see anyone on my way out of the house to the wedding site, either. Well, it wouldn't matter if I ran into Charles again, since he's the only person who knows what I'm wearing. He found all the pieces for me in the costume shop. "It's all yours," he said. "None of it's been worn since *Shrew* closed. But don't worry, it *has* all been washed."

I pull on the hose, button the doublet, slide on the buckled shoes, and put on the high-crowned hat. Now I'm ready to go witness the marriage of Aurora and Robert, dressed as, depending on your point of view, either Petruchio or my brother.

ACT V

I Got Lucky

scene i

AURORA AND ROBERT'S friends' barn is about forty-five minutes outside of Portland, where gas stations and strip malls give way to feed stores and tree farms, and everyone on the road seems to think that seventy is the right speed to take blind turns. It's cooler outside of the city, maybe because there are even more trees, and the sky is full of gray clouds. I follow the signs for the Kneedler/Cracknell wedding and park at the side of what I first think is just a small gravel road, but then realize is an extremely long driveway.

More signs guide me to the barn, which has garlands of ivy hung over the doorway. A crowd is gathered around a giant oak tree not far from the barn, and the first person I recognize is Henry, who looks remarkably distinguished—the fashion-conscious ogre, again—in a jacket, tie, and kilt.

As I get closer, I see that it's easy to tell the difference between Aurora's and Robert's friends. Robert's are all guys, and they come in two body types: tall, ponytailed, and weedy or short, stocky, and bearded. They all look like the last time they willingly wore a costume—or anything other than a T-shirt and jeans—was sometime in elementary school. Most of them are dressed as pirates, or at least approximations thereof. I find this a little surprising, until I notice that Charles—shirtless, in black leather shorts and combat boots, covered in body paint that matches his blue hair—is holding a large grocery bag full of eye patches and bandanas, which he's distributing to anyone who doesn't look quite costumed enough.

Aurora's friends, of course, are all over the map, in more ways than one—I wouldn't want to guess the gender of more than half of them. But there are some themes among their costumes. Anything that can be cantilevered to feature cleavage is popular: mermaids, belly dancers, saucy tavern wenches, devil girls, angels, witches, fairies, and costumes-that-are-only-costumes-because-there's-a-mask-but-otherwise-it's-just-a-halter-top-and-a-miniskirt. More masculine costumes include cops, firefighters, cowboys, bikers, Mexican wrestlers, a gladiator whose outfit is made from what appears to be an old leather suitcase, and a few more pirates, but pirates who look dirtier, shabbier, and altogether more authentically piratical than Robert's reluctant friends.

After a while, I catch sight of Damian, who looks absolutely comfortable and natural in Middle Eastern robes.

"Hey!" A firefighter I've never met before claps me on the back. "Looking good, dude!"

I smile and say nothing.

"Yeah," the firefighter continues, "some of us were talking about getting a game together after. You up?"

I shrug. "We'll see," I say, trying to pitch my voice low.

Just then, a bell rings, and then I hear, unmistakably, a marching band. They burst out of the barn wearing red and gold, looking like a demented halftime show, sounding like their goal is to raise whatever dead might be buried underneath the oak tree. There are only about a dozen of them, but they sound like three times that many, playing a fast swing arrangement of what I eventually recognize as David Bowie's "Modern Love." They're marching toward Henry, who's standing directly underneath the tree.

The crowd parts for the band as it promenades and miraculously splits itself into more-or-less equal clumps, forming a central aisle. Across the aisle I spot Meryl, a mermaid today. Then she sees me and her eyes widen, and I wonder if she thinks I'm Nick, too. I haven't seen him yet.

I shiver. It's definitely much cooler here than it was in the city, and the sky keeps getting more gray. One good thing about my costume is that it's significantly warmer than what a lot of other people are wearing.

The band forms itself into a loose square to Henry's left, continuing to play at maximum volume. Then comes the little boy who's playing the changeling in the show, tossing huge handfuls of rose petals onto the ground from a purple satin bag. Then Robert, wearing a dark brown suit that doesn't look like any sort of costume, except maybe I Have a Job Interview.

And finally Aurora.

If I hadn't had art history last year, I wouldn't have known that she looks like a painting by Dante Gabriel Rossetti. A specific one—I forget the name, but it's a black-haired woman in drapey amber silk. In the painting, the woman looks contemptuous and a little bored, but here in reality, Aurora is glowing.

The band plays one last flourish, and then Henry clears his throat and begins to speak.

What he says is nothing like what my father says at weddings, but the mood, somehow, is the same: solemn and happy in equal parts.

It makes me sad, though. I can't help thinking that there's no way I'll ever be looking at someone the way Aurora's looking at Robert, while someone like Henry talks about "the secret sympathy, the silver link, the silken tie."

But then I remind myself of how much Aurora and Robert have been through—so much that I'm not even aware of—to get to where they are now, and I think, well, you never know.

Then the middle-school fairies—or rather, Delirium, Arwen, Revolutionary Girl Utena, and some other anime character I don't recognize but whose costume includes goggles, a dark green cloak, and a big stuffed rabbit—appear from behind the marching band. They start to sing Titania's lullaby, their voices blending in close harmony. They sound younger than they look, and otherworldly. If I close my eyes, I can almost make myself believe that they *are* fairies, warning the spiders, snakes, and beetles away from their queen.

When they finish, there's silence, then the vows and the exchange of rings, which are three-dollar hematite rings from a hippie store in the neighborhood where I canvass. I know this because I saw Robert right after he bought them. He was in such a good mood that he signed my petition.

Just as Henry is pronouncing Aurora and Robert married, and telling them to kiss, it starts to rain, in big spattery sheets, just like last night.

They kiss for a long time, and people applaud, scream, and hoot. Finally someone yells, "All right already, you want us all to get hit by lightning?"

They break the kiss, laugh, then, holding hands, run back down the aisle we've made toward the barn, and after a token second or so, everyone else follows them.

The barn looks like it's been several decades since it's been used for its original purpose. It's scrupulously clean and well lit, with dozens of strings of tiny white Christmas lights along the walls. There's a full bar, a huge buffet of food from the Lebanese restaurant, lots of folding chairs and little round tables with white tablecloths. Even with all that, there's still some space for dancing. And in one corner, plugged, along with the Christmas lights, into what I guess must be a generator, are a television and a karaoke machine.

"Oh my God!" I hear Damian shriek. "Make way for the Karaoke Master!"

Soon the guests have split into three groups—the line for the food, the line for drinks, and the line for karaoke. I decide that my top priority is to avoid the firefighter who thinks I'm Nick, but since there are several firefighters in attendance, it's a bit challenging. I see one walking in my direction, and I duck outside, where Meryl and several other smokers are huddling under a geisha's parasol, trying to light their cigarettes in the rain. Meryl has her arm around the geisha, who is tiny and androgynous. I turn around and head back inside.

Nick is in the line for karaoke. He's dressed as, depending on your point of view, either a minister, or our father.

I stand in the doorway for a minute, not sure where I should go, or if maybe I should just leave. That's when Henry reaches out, pulls me inside, and hugs me. "Hey, kiddo," he says. "Nice costume."

"Thanks," I say. "You knew it was me right away?"

Henry laughs. "Well, the clothes look familiar, but honey, no way are those boy legs." He looks at my legs and smiles.

"Were you in that show, too?"

He nods. "Christopher Sly."

"You were really good today."

"Well, thank you. You know I enjoy exercising my authority."

I laugh, and we get into the line for drinks, acquire beers, and sit at one of the little tables. After a minute or so, Charles joins us. "I can't stay," he says. "I still have a few things to finish up back at the theater."

"Ah, don't worry about it," says Henry. "You think anyone else is going to get any work done today?" He waves his arm around the room.

Charles smiles. "You may be right. But the other thing is that after a while, this body paint itches like you would not believe."

But he doesn't leave, and we all sit and talk about nothing in particular, and Henry and I have a few more beers, and then in the karaoke line, Nick's up, and he launches into "I Walk the Line."

"Oh, come on," I hear myself say. "That's not the right song. Try 'The Gambler,' why don't you?"

Charles and Henry look at me.

"Sorry. Nothing."

And then Meryl lurches into the chair next to me. "But you're over there," she says fuzzily, pointing at Nick, who's now imploring all and sundry to stay together, in the words of Al Green.

"Glad to know I'm so *memorable*," I say.

She blinks. "Oh," she says, light dawning. "It's you."

"Does it matter?" I ask.

"Why're you being so mean?" she asks. "And before, why'd you *leave*?"

I don't have a good answer for her, so I don't say anything.

Charles takes the silence as his cue to leave, but Henry stays put, and I'm glad.

"You just *left*," she says.

She's still damp from the sudden storm and looks even more mermaidlike as a result. I know just how her slick skin would feel against mine.

But I don't reach for her.

Henry taps her on the shoulder and says, "Miss Meryl. May I have this dance?"

And they dance, like mermaid Beauty and a Scottish Beast, to a slow song from the marching band, subdued and stationary now, with mutes on their horns. I see that Robert and Aurora are dancing, too. There's a cowboy with a Mexican wrestler. A fairy and a witch. Revolutionary Girl Utena and Damian. It's clear that many of these dance partners aren't couples in real life. Just because two of the people in this barn have decided to spend their lives together doesn't mean the rest of us are obligated to instantly find our soul mates. It's okay if we just dance.

I get up, and join the other dancers.

HOURS LATER, the rain has stopped, and the crowd has thinned out to those of us who said we'd stay to help clean up. Nick vanished a while ago, along with the firefighter, a cowboy, and a devil girl. We exchanged no words before he left. Aurora and Robert are long gone, too. They're not having a real honeymoon until the show closes, of course, but they've got a hotel room for tonight.

Henry and Meryl, somewhat to my surprise, have stuck around, too. Meryl hasn't made any more attempts to talk about what is or is not happening with the two of us, but I haven't really given her the opportunity, either. According to Nic, I'm "the queen of being unavailable for processing."

What happened with Nic and me? It came down to two things: us living too far apart, and my not being good at talking the way Nic thought people should talk when they were In a Relationship. Or maybe three: the third being that anytime either of us tried to be sexy on the phone or, worse, over IM, we'd get giggly, embarrassed, or both. So now she and I are friends—not with benefits, but with memories. Although who's to say what would happen if we were in the same place again? I let myself think about it for a minute, then shake my head to clear it, and get to work.

It takes us about an hour to make the barn look like a barn again. Then Nancy, one of the barn's owners, makes everyone coffee and tells us that if anyone's not in shape to drive back into town, they've got crash space. A few people take her up on it.

"Oh, shit!" Meryl says. "Charles left, didn't he?"

"Yeah, a while ago."

"Hmm, I think Damian's departed as well," Henry says. So of course I offer to give them both a ride back.

The drive seems shorter going back into Portland. Henry's riding shotgun. Meryl is fast asleep, sprawled across the backseat, with Henry's jacket draped over her as a blanket.

"That one's a candle-at-both-ends type, but you're not," Henry says quietly.

I shrug. "I don't know."

"I get the sense you're used to handling a lot and keeping it together."

"Maybe I'm just waiting for the right moment to fall apart."

"Maybe," Henry says, "but I don't think so. For an actress, you have an underdeveloped sense of personal drama."

"You think I'm an actress?"

"I think you can act. Whether you stay an actress, of course, is up to you."

"Acting does kind of run in my family," I say. Even Mom, who was never in a show that I can remember, spent a lot of time on the puppets from our old puppet stage.

"But not everything does," Henry says, suddenly very serious-sounding. "You need to remember that."

BY THE TIME I pull up in front of Forest House, it feels like at least four in the morning, but it's not even midnight. Henry's still in the car because he says he doesn't mind taking the bus home, and it's a good thing, too, because we can't get Meryl to wake up, so Henry carries her to the doorway like she's a little kid.

When I open the door, Henry and I are confronted by the sight of all the costumes from the costume shop, draped over every surface in the living room. There are lots of candles burning, too, some scented, and the cloying vanilla/patchouli/honey mixes with the usual combination of plants, books, and mildew. There's another scent, too—mothballs—and it dawns on me that all the costumes are wet.

"The costume shop got flooded," Charles says. He's standing over one of the fairy costumes. I can just barely discern that he's also no longer blue, except for his hair and a few spots on his face and neck, and he's wearing regular clothes. "I moved everything over here after I found out."

"Oh, God, Charles, you did that all by yourself?" I ask.

"I managed to get hold of some of the Minions. They're back at the theater working on cleaning things up there. I tried to reach Nick, but I guess he forgot to charge his phone again. What happened to Meryl?"

At the mention of her name, Meryl stirs, looking confused. She blinks, and Henry sets her gently onto her feet.

"What the hell?" Meryl asks. "What—wait." She rubs her eyes. "Nothing happened to me. I was just asleep. God, what a mess."

"Well, we do seem to have ourselves a situation here," Henry says.

"Wait . . . is there some reason you can't just put them in the dryer?" Meryl asks.

"The power's out, remember? Or did you think I was just in a romantic mood?" Charles asks, gesturing at the candles.

"Shit, I did forget. But hold on! There are some drying racks in the basement—those would at least be better than using the furniture—and I think the wringer Aurora found at that one estate sale is down there, too."

Meryl's nap must have given her energy. She grabs a candle and heads for the basement, walking awkwardly because of her tight green fishtail skirt. Then her voice carries up the stairs: "Hey, guess where else is flooded?"

"Oh, that's just fucking fabulous. How bad?" Charles calls.

"Bring buckets."

There are no buckets to be found, but after a few minutes, Henry, Charles, and I clomp down the stairs to the basement, Charles with a stockpot, Henry with a saucepan, and me with a candle in each hand.

The water's only about half an inch deep. It wouldn't be so bad, if not for the fact that the basement is crammed with rusty bicycles, broken furniture, old magazines, stacks of cardboard boxes, garbage bags full of clothing. The mildew scent is even stronger down here.

"*Damn* it, look at this," Meryl says.

She hands her candle to me and starts to lift a cardboard box, the bottom of which is soaked through.

"Careful, you don't know what—" Charles starts.

The bottom of the box gives way and a big, bright pink glass serving dish falls to the wet concrete floor and shatters.

"Don't say it," Meryl says. She takes a step back from the shards, then grimaces. "Helpful tip: when it breaks, glass travels quite a distance. Oh, *ow*." She lifts her right foot off the floor.

There's blood streaming from a spot near the ball of her foot.

"Oh, Jesus Christ. I *so* did not need this," Charles says.

"*You* didn't?" Meryl asks, through clenched teeth.

Charles sighs. "Sorry." He turns to me. "Wait. You are

wearing one of the only undamaged costumes I have left. I am not going to let you ruin it slogging through this mess. So you're going to go change, but first you're going to help Meryl upstairs and see how bad her foot is. You might need to get her to the emergency room. Henry, if you don't mind, help me do some triage down here?"

He kicks at the remnants of the cardboard box, then scoops up some water into his stockpot. Henry says, "If you can find a mop, I'm your man, but I'll warn you that my knees aren't up to a lot of stooping and bailing."

"Don't move," I say to Meryl. "We don't know where all the glass went. If you take another step you might cut yourself again. I think I'm going to have to carry you."

"Jesus. Everyone's just dragging me around today."

"Shut up." I hand the candles to Henry. "Go in front of us so we can see our way up the stairs."

"Wait," Meryl says. She fishes inside the nearest garbage bag and comes up with a ragged T-shirt, then wraps it around her foot. "There. Charles, look. I'm making sure no blood will get on Battle's costume."

Then I bend down, and she wraps her arms around my neck.

The Petruchio shoes have slippery soles. If we were in a horror movie, this is when Henry would reveal himself as the psychopath. But he doesn't, of course. He walks in front of us with the candles, making two quivering pools of light, as I slide my way along the wet floor, back to the steps.

Halfway up, I have to stop, panting.

"Sorry. Clearly I shouldn't have had so much baba ghanoush," Meryl says. "Oh, *fuck*, my foot hurts."

"It's fine. Just give me a second. Okay. Here we go again."

On the step second from the top, my foot slips. I reach out for the banister, and it creaks ominously and comes away a little from the wall, but holds.

"Made it."

I bend my knees again so Meryl can get down without putting weight on her cut foot.

Henry hands me one of the candles. "I'm heading back down to help Charles. You okay to take it from here?"

I nod. Meryl says, "You should still bring up those drying racks, and the wringer. Oh, *ow*."

I kneel beside Meryl and give her the candle. "Hold this, so I can take a look at that cut." I take her injured foot in my hands and unwind the T-shirt. "We're gonna have to wash the blood off before I'll be able to see the shard, I think. It must be really tiny."

"Doesn't *feel* tiny."

"I know. But can you lift your foot up to the sink?"

"Yeah, but I'd rather not," Meryl says, eyeing the sink. The candle provides enough light for us to see that it's full of dirty dishes.

"Oh, God, sorry, gross—I'll move them."

I stack bowls and plates haphazardly on the counter, then turn on the faucet. Meryl sticks the candle into a juice glass.

"Hold on to my leg in case I have trouble balancing," she says. "The counter's so high, it's like doing the splits standing up."

She unzips her mermaid skirt and wriggles out of it, revealing that she's wearing bike shorts underneath. Practical.

As we stand there, me holding on to Meryl's thigh while she runs her foot under the cold water, the back door opens and Nick walks in. He looks us up and down and says, "Now *that's* an innovative approach."

"She's hurt," I snap. "The basement is flooded. So is the costume shop. The power's still out, as you might have noticed. Charles tried calling you. Where the fuck have you *been*?"

"I got lucky."

"I don't want to know."

"Not like that, please, how vulgar. I mean, I got Lucky."

He opens the back porch door wider, and there, tied to a tree, is the little beige dog.

I feel like I've been punched in the stomach. I let go of Meryl's leg and stare out into the backyard. Lucky barks.

"Still bleeding," Meryl says softly. She lowers her leg to the floor and her face creases as the blood returns to her foot.

"Damn!" Nick says. "That looks serious!"

"Why, yes," Meryl says, "shards of glass lodged in flesh usually are."

"Okay." I put my hands on Nick's shoulders. "Right now, I'm going to drive Meryl to the emergency room. *Do not leave*, for any reason. There's still dog food up in my room—"

"I know, that's where I got the leash!"

"Okay," I say again. "When I get back, you and I are going to talk. In the meantime, clean up the blood, then help Henry and Charles, and then wash the damn dishes."

Nick opens his mouth, shuts it again. Then he rips several paper towels off the roll, sprays them with the bottle of glass cleaner that's next to the sink, gets on his knees, and starts to clean the blood from the floor.

"I can't afford the emergency room," Meryl says.

"Don't worry about it," I say.

"No—"

"Shut up. We're going."

"You have to change first, remember?"

Ten minutes for me to run upstairs, hit my head on one of the hanging planters on the way up, rip off my Petruchio-wear, throw on a T-shirt and jeans, realize I should get regular clothes for Meryl, too, dive into the morass that is her room, locate a shirt, a skirt, and flip-flops, and run back downstairs. Two more minutes for her to pull the shirt over her head, the skirt over her hips. We wrap the T-shirt around her hurt foot again, for lack of anything better, then she has to sit down to slide one flip-flop onto her noninjured foot. Finally we make it back out to my car, slowly, with Meryl hopping, and again she sprawls across the backseat, wide awake this time.

"I CAN'T BELIEVE how dumb that was," Meryl says in the ER. "If I can't walk—I mean, what if I need crutches? I'll ruin the show."

"No, you'll just be on crutches."

"It'll be a disaster."

"So what if it is? Didn't y'all have any disasters during *Taming of the Shrew*?"

Meryl smiles. "Yeah, come to think of it. One."

We're silent for a while, and then Meryl says, "So. What's up with you?"

"What do you mean?"

"I mean what's your *deal*?"

"In what sense?"

"*God* you're annoying."

"Sorry."

"'Sorry' doesn't quite make it. You chase after me starting the day you got here, you make your first move in the parking lot of the *gun range*, you blow God knows how much cash getting my piece-of-shit truck fixed, you refuse to take no for an answer, and when you're finally, you know, wearing me down some, you just fucking disappear?"

I note that we're providing entertainment for everyone else in the waiting room. A mouth-breathing guy who's done something awful to his hand—it's wrapped in a bloody T-shirt, the bandage of choice for emergency-room visits—is looking especially interested.

"Could we maybe not talk about this right now?"

"When *else* are we going to talk about it?"

I think of a cartoon I once saw that has a guy looking at his datebook: *How about never? Is never good for you?*

But what I say is, "I guess I just, you know, I think you're right, you know, about you being older and more experienced, and stuff."

"Oh, so now I'm some battered old skank?"

See, *this* is why I can't have these kinds of conversations. If I ever give in and say something, it always comes out wrong. I try to bail myself out.

"Well, it's just, you know, I'm going to be starting school soon, too, and you know what that's like."

"No, I don't, actually," she says. "Unless you mean what it's like to scrape together the cash for a class at the community college, knowing that you've had to drop the last three times because of your work schedule, and that at this rate, you'll get your associate's degree around your fortieth birthday."

"I just mean I know I'm going to be busy, okay?"

And then, thank God, the nurse calls Meryl's name.

*   *   *

WHEN SHE EMERGES, two and a half hours later, Meryl is on crutches, and her foot is swathed in bandages.

"I'm not supposed to put weight on it for a week," she says.

"I'm sorry."

Not just about the crutches, but I'm not sure if she understands that.

"I'll bring the car around," I say.

It takes me a while to find it. Once I'm inside, I shiver. I can't tell whether it's from cold, fatigue, or worry. I rub my eyes, then start the engine and make my way back to the entrance, where Meryl's waiting. She climbs in, gingerly.

"I still can't believe it," Meryl says, looking at her bandaged foot.

Images flash in my mind—the drift of unopened bills on the closet floor, Lucky tied to the tree, Nick kneeling to wipe up Meryl's blood—and I say, "Neither can I."

THE FIRST THING I hear when we get back is Lucky, crying. He's still tied to the tree. Nick's nowhere in sight. At least he left the food and water dishes within Lucky's reach.

"*Damn* it," I say.

I get out of the car and go over to untie him. Meryl follows me, slowly, on her crutches.

Lucky jumps up and puts his paws on my knees. I pet

him, and he licks my hands and face. I have to smile.

"Are you surprised?" Meryl asks.

"He could still be in the basement helping Henry and Charles."

"Yeah, that's likely."

"Shut up. You should go to bed. Put your foot up. Get some rest."

"What were you going to talk to him about?"

I say to Lucky, "You're *so* good. Yes you are. Yes."

Henry steps out onto the back porch and stretches. He looks tired. "Oh, good, you two made it back. How's that foot?"

Meryl says, "Oh, God, Henry, I can't put any weight on it. Aurora's going to kill me. All the blocking—I don't know what we're going to do. God, I'm such a fuckup!"

She starts to cry.

Henry gives her a hug. "It's okay, honey. You didn't hurt your foot on purpose. We'll figure out some new blocking."

"Where's Nick?" I ask.

"Up the street, picking up some pizza—I don't know about you two, but everyone here is ravenous. That cleanup job was murder. Come on inside. You need to put your foot up, Miss Meryl."

Henry opens the door for Meryl. After she limps in, before he shuts the door, he looks over at me, still kneeling, still petting Lucky. "That's a nice dog," he says. "Same one you found in traffic?"

"Yeah."

"He get out again?"

"I don't know. Nick brought him over."

"Hmm," Henry says. "Don't stay out there too long. You don't want to miss out on the food."

After a few minutes, I tie Lucky up again and come in, and see that the kitchen's full of people. It reminds me of that Marx Brothers movie where they're on an ocean liner, and everyone ends up in Groucho's tiny cabin. Nick's come back with the pizza, and Henry, Meryl, Damian, Charles, and some of the Minions have already dug in. I didn't think I was hungry, but the overpowering scent makes me grab a couple of slices.

Everyone's punchy and loud. There's an edge in people's voices, and the laughter sounds a little manic. But a few sensible decisions are being made. The costumes that aren't too fragile to be put in a dryer are getting divided up among the cast and crew who have access to functional machines. Meryl's going to call Aurora and Robert in the morning—"So at least they get to have a wedding night"—to let them know she's now on crutches, so Aurora will have the maximum amount of time to think about new blocking. One of the Minions knows how to rent a Dumpster, to get rid of everything that was ruined. I eat my pizza without saying anything, letting it all wash over me.

"So, you wanted to talk to me about something?" Nick reaches over, grabs a crust from my plate, and takes a big bite.

I snatch it back. "You know that's my favorite part."

"You weren't eating it."

"I was saving it."

"Sorry. But what did you want to talk about? I'm all ears." He smiles.

Moments before, the kitchen had been a babble of voices. But now, one of the inexplicable silences that always seem to happen in groups falls. Everyone looks at me.

"I—I just wanted to thank you. For getting Lucky back."

"Ah—it's the least I could do. You know, I saw him out in the street again, that's why I did it. I went over there . . ." His voice changes. It's low, but perfectly audible—he's playing to the crowd. "I went over there and I said, 'Look. It seems like you're a little overwhelmed, taking care of this animal. I mean, he's been running around loose in heavy traffic on at least three occasions that I know of, and that's very dangerous. Now my sister is very, very good with dogs, and I *know* she will give him an excellent home.'" He flashes me a smile.

"What about that little boy? The one who was so happy when you brought Lucky back before?"

Nick waves his arm dismissively. "He was playing a video game."

"Did you *pay* them?"

He grins, then takes the crust I was saving again.

This time I let him.

The Minions start talking about who had the hottest costumes at the wedding, and the crazy stuff they found clearing out the basement. "Damn, I don't even *wanna* know whose, like, *apparatus* that was down there. That shit was seriously kinky."

Aurora's antique wringer?

Meryl looks at me like maybe she wants to talk more, or something, but I look away, then go out to Lucky again. He rests his head on my knee. I scratch him behind the ears.

"Hey, sweet little doggie. What am I gonna do with you, huh? I'll be in a dorm room pretty soon. I don't think they let dogs stay in dorms. But maybe I can hide you. How're you doing, little guy? Do you miss your other people?"

I look into Lucky's shiny black eyes, but they don't tell me anything.

Then Meryl limps out, lowers herself onto the porch step, and lights a cigarette.

"You need to know something," she says.

Oh, God, what else? Did Nick get her pregnant and not pay for the abortion?

"I don't always want things to turn into sex." She inhales, then exhales smoke through her nose. "But I don't know what to do when they don't."

Last year I told Nic that words don't always work.

Some things don't change.

I look up at Meryl, nod, and half smile.

She nods back, puts out her cigarette, and limps back inside.

scene ii

THE NEXT DAY, I have to work until rehearsal, so I don't see Nick or Meryl until I get to the theater.

And rehearsal—dress rehearsal—is a disaster.

The light cues are out of sync.

The new blocking that we worked out at the last minute to accommodate Meryl throws everyone off.

Demetrius trips over one of Meryl's crutches.

Annalisa gets the hiccups during her "These are the forgeries of jealousy" speech, which causes her daughter and the rest of the middle-school fairies to giggle uncontrollably for the remainder of the scene.

One of the tree-columns falls and hits Henry on the head.

Alone onstage for the final speech of the show, Nick says, "Gentles, if we have offended—thank your stars, the show has ended."

"ALL RIGHT, EVERYONE. I know you don't need me to tell you that tonight was rough." Aurora runs her hands through her hair and sighs.

"It's no wonder. Mercury is retrograde," Annalisa says.

"'The fault, dear Brutus, is not in our stars but in ourselves,'" Henry quotes. "Have I got a lump on top of my head?"

"No," Aurora says. "Listen, folks. Despite everything that happened tonight, you've all been working very hard. I have every confidence that it will come together tomorrow for opening. I do have a few notes, but I'm going to keep them short."

After Aurora finishes, there's a general consensus to go to the Russian restaurant that stays open late.

"I can't," I say. "I have to walk the dog."

I KNEEL FOR a minute, petting Lucky. "Okay, sweet doggie. I'm gonna take you for a nice long walk, but there's something I have to do first."

I tie Lucky up and go inside. From the kitchen I take a wastebasket, a flashlight, a book of matches, and a knife.

* * *

I SHINE THE flashlight onto Nick's closet floor. The snow-drift of unpaid bills is still there, still untouched.

I scoop them up and dump them onto Nick's futon, then squat on the futon next to the pile. By the light of the flash-light, I sort the bills into stacks: electricity, phone, water, gas, credit card. Then I sort each stack by date.

When I have the most recent version of each bill, I throw the older ones into the wastebasket.

So far, the process feels hypnotic, almost soothing.

I pick up the knife and slice open the remaining enve-lopes.

I'm good at math. Algebra, geometry, calculus, trig—none of them faze me.

This is just simple arithmetic.

I take my checkbook out of my back pocket.

Before I finish writing the first check, I'm crying.

By the time I write the last one, I'm shaking.

I realize that if I'm going to mail all these checks off, I'll need stamps.

But what I have left, after writing all these checks, is thirty-three cents.

And this, finally, is what sends me over the edge, or maybe back *from* the edge, to decide that I am not, after all, going to spend my college tuition money to clear my brother's gambling debts. I slide open the green box, place the most recent version of each bill inside, and slide it shut.

Then I go through the checks.

VOID, I write. VOID. VOID. VOID. VOID. VOID.

"LUCKY, I'M SORRY, sweetie, but you're going to have to wait just a little bit longer."

I set the wastebasket down. It's metal, and it makes a satisfying clang on the concrete walk.

I strike a match and throw it into the basket.

The old bills, and my checks, flare up quickly. To make sure they don't get caught up and carried away by the wind, I weigh them down with a few fallen branches.

I look into the flames and see the word *Power*, a scrap from one of the electric bills. Then the corner of the paper curls up and dissolves into ashes, and it's gone.

"What the hell are you doing? Is there something burning in there? I thought you were walking the dog."

Meryl gets out of Henry's car, and after a minute, so does Henry.

"I'm just about to," I say. I rub my eyes, trying to remove the traces of tears.

Meryl limps over to the wastebasket.

"I know tonight sucked, but setting your script on fire seems a little over the top."

I start to laugh.

Henry comes over and puts a hand on my shoulder.

"Anything I can do?"

I stop laughing. I look into Henry's kind eyes and nod.

"Come with me while I walk the dog."

"I see how it is," Meryl says. "All this time, you were really just looking for an older man."

"Meryl, I—"

"Kidding! Learn to take a joke, why don't you?" She pokes me in the leg with a crutch.

"Okay," I say. "I'll work on that."

Meryl crutches away and into the house. Henry and I watch as the bills and checks burn themselves out in the wastebasket.

"So, you want to talk about it, kiddo?"

If anyone but Henry had called me that, I would've wanted to punch them.

"It's complicated."

"I figured. Shall we walk?"

I nod, and get the dog. The dog—something else I don't know what I'm going to do about.

We wait while Lucky sniffs a tree, then lifts his leg to mark it.

"That book you loaned me," I say. "I was irritated with the main character, what was his name again?"

"Dunstan."

"Right, Dunstan. For the longest time I couldn't understand why anybody would feel so responsible for something that obviously wasn't their fault."

"Hmm," Henry says. "And?"

"And then, I don't know. It just started to feel real."

Henry nods. "Well, and I think part of what makes the book work so well is that Boy isn't heartless. He's just thoughtless. He believes that he has Dunstan's best interests at heart. But is literature really what you want to talk about, honey?"

"Not exactly. I guess."

We walk some more. I yank Lucky away from the remains of someone's fried chicken.

"Might I be so bold as to speculate that this has something to do with a blood relation of yours?"

I nod, and I'm crying again. But what if Henry tells Aurora and Robert, and gets Nick kicked out of Forest House?

Not that he doesn't deserve it.

I dig into my pocket and bring out the small green box. "Do you know what this is?"

Henry holds it up to the streetlight we're walking under. "How'd you come by it?"

"Don't open it. Could you just tell me what it is?"

Henry hands it back to me. "If it's what it looks like, it's an antique, and it's called a tell box."

"What do you use it for?"

"Cheating at cards."

I rub my eyes.

"How are your parents, honey?" Henry asks, not at all what I thought he would say. "Are they together?"

"They're not divorced."

"What I mean is, can you tell them?"

scene iii

THE NEXT DAY, I have to work again until call.

I don't know how I get through the day.

And I *really* don't know how the show manages to come together, but somehow, miraculously, it does.

Nick, especially, is stunning.

I find him just outside the men's dressing room after I wash off my makeup and change. His is still on.

"You were great. Really fantastic."

"So were you." Nick hugs me.

Still in his arms, I take a deep breath. "But we need to talk now."

He lets go of me and takes a step away.

I hand him the tell box. "Open it."

"How did you—?" He slides it open, sees the bills. Then he

puts his head in his hands. When he looks up, his makeup is streaked with tears.

I applaud.

"Stop."

"You know I have to tell Mom and Dad," I say.

We look at each other.

Nick wipes his eyes with the back of his hand. Then he shakes his head, and clears his throat. "No. Let me."

That's when Charles comes up and says that everyone's meeting at the Russian restaurant to celebrate, but before we go, Aurora and Robert want to get all the housemates together in the costume shop for an announcement.

My heart rate skyrockets. I'm convinced that the announcement will be, "We've discovered that Nick is screwing us over."

"He can't have knocked her up already," my brother says.

Charles punches Nick lightly on the arm. "Not funny. Come on."

"This will just take a minute, then we can join the others down the street," Aurora says. "And I'm sorry to just pull you all in here like this. But we wanted to give you as much notice as possible, because we know this is going to come as a shock—"

"Let me cut to the chase," Robert says. "We're going to sell the house."

"So, I know that it's not going to be an issue for *you*,

Battle," Aurora says, patting my hand. "I know you were going to be moving out soon in *any* case, but all you others, you're going to need to start looking for new places to live."

Charles whistles. "End of an era."

"I know," Aurora says. "But we agreed, we need a place that's *ours*, just ours." Robert nods.

"How soon do you need us out?" Meryl asks.

"Oh, well, goodness, not *immediately*, certainly," Aurora says.

"Good," says my brother, "because some of us will have a few things to deal with. Loose ends. You know."

Robert looks at him.

"But we *are* going to need to get Forest House in shape to be *shown*, you know, and that's going to mean making a lot of changes—"

"You'll get thirty days," Robert says.

"Good!" Nick says again. "Since that's the law." I can't believe how righteous he sounds.

"Thanks for not waiting to tell us. I'll miss Forest House, but it totally makes sense that you two would want to sell and get a place by yourselves. Being the den mother was getting a little tired, huh?" Charles, ever the diplomat, smiles at Aurora. "So," he goes on, "now that that's settled, let's go celebrate a *fantastic* performance."

And we do.

scene iii

NICK DOESN'T EVEN want me to be there when he calls
Mom and Dad, but his phone is disconnected for nonpay-
ment, so he has to use mine.

We place the call in my room, and I make him put it on
speakerphone. This means that I can clearly hear Mom's
sharp intake of breath, and a little later, her sobs. I wouldn't
have needed the speakerphone to hear Dad, though.

As for Nick—I thought he was good as Puck. But com-
pared to this perfomance, that was nothing.

After forever, Mom and Dad want to talk to me.

"I don't understand why you didn't tell us sooner." Mom.

"We expect better from you." Dad.

But not from Nick.

scene iv

THE RUN OF *Midsummer* passes in fast-forward. When we're
not onstage or at work, all of us at Forest House are making
plans. It looks like Charles will be able to sublet a room in the
house where Damian's living. One of the Minions is moving

out of a studio that Meryl thinks she can afford if she picks up some more hours at the pool. Aurora and Robert are combing the house listings and arguing about craftsmen and ranches and bedrooms and garages. I'm IMing a lot with my soon-to-be roommate, a girl named Kristine. She's from Sacramento, and she'll be getting into town next week. We go back and forth about what we think we're going to need for our room, and what we're allowed to have. She really loves dogs, she told me.

And Nick?

After the show closes, he's going to move back to Chapel Hill and live with our parents. Henry, Meryl, and Charles have all, separately, asked me what I think about this. I told them all the same thing: "I'm just glad I'm not going to be back there until Thanksgiving."

scene v

NICK AND I are standing in the train station, and he's about to board.

He kneels, opens his suitcase. "For you." He hands me the tell box. "It's empty now."

Because Mom and Dad are bailing him out, I know. And

how thoughtful, to make *me* the one to return what he stole.

That's Nick.

I smile. "Thanks. And hold on, I've got a present for you, too."

"Should I be worried?" he asks.

"No. It used to be yours. I'm just giving it back." I reach into my bag and bring out the boy puppet. Mom made him for Nick, back when we were little.

"Oh, my God," Nick says. "I can't believe you still have this! That's so great, thank you! But wait, wasn't there—didn't he have a little crown, or something, before?"

I shrug. "I just thought you should have him."

"Take care of yourself," he says, then gives me a hug.

"You, too."

I know he will.

LATER THAT DAY, before I meet Kristine for coffee, I'm walking Lucky to the dog park, and picturing Nick on the train.

He'll have a window seat. He'll be looking out, watching the landscape shift. Or maybe he'll be talking to the person next to him. If he is—and I can picture that, too, his conspiratorial tone, his smile—he'll make them feel special. Chosen.

I bend down, pick a dandelion, and blow the seeds into the air. Lucky strains at his leash.

"I know," I say. "You just can't wait, can you, sweetie?"

We go up a gentle slope and enter the off-leash area. I kneel and unhook Lucky's leash from his collar. He wags his tail, quivering all over.

"Okay," I say. "Go!"

And Lucky flings himself forward, running like leashes have never been invented, like his ridiculous little legs can carry him anywhere.

a c k n o w l e d g m e n t s

Thanks to

everyone who's written to me about *Empress*
and wanted to know when this book was coming

all of my friends

Jacqui, who knows why

Mom and Dad,
who are nothing at all like Battle's parents

Sharyn, always

Sara Ryan is also the author of *Empress of the World*, which was named an ALA Best Book for Young Adults, a *Booklist* Top Ten Teen Romance, and a Lambda Award Finalist, and won the Oregon Book Award.

She and cartoonist Steve Lieber collaborated on the short comics *Flytrap: Juggling Act* and *Me and Edith Head*. The latter, which featured a character from *Empress of the World*, was an Eisner Award Finalist for Best Short Story. She lives in Portland, Oregon.

Visit her Web site at **www.sararyan.com**.